THE
EXECUTIONER'S
GAME

GARY HARDWICK

HarperTorch
An Imprint of HarperCollinsPublishers

HARPERTORCH
An Imprint of HarperCollins*Publishers*
10 East 53rd Street
New York, New York 10022-5299

Copyright © 2005 by Gary Hardwick
ISBN 13: 978-0-06-057585-4
ISBN: 0-06-057585-9

First HarperTorch paperback printing: January 2006
First William Morrow hardcover printing: January 2005

HarperCollins®, HarperTorch™, and ◆™ are trademarks of HarperCollins Publishers Inc.

Printed in the United States of America

Visit HarperTorch on the World Wide Web at
www.harpercollins.com

10 9 8 7 6 5 4 3 2 1

To my paternal grandfather,

George Hardwick

Whenever the people shall grow weary of the existing government, they can exercise their constitutional right of amending it, or their revolutionary right to dismember or overthrow it.

—Abraham Lincoln, first inaugural
address, March 4, 1861

The only freedom consists in the people taking care of the government.

—Woodrow Wilson,
address, September 4, 1912

You can go home again, but the house is on fire.

—Joe Black, 2004

THE
EXECUTIONER'S
GAME

SHADOW GAME

When executing an assignment, an operative must place the success of the mission above all other concerns, including the lives of nonoperatives, cooperatives, and the operative himself.

—E-1 Operations Mission Manual, Rule 1

Africa

It was a bad sun. That's what the locals said. It wasn't customary to think of the sun as something capable of negative energy, but you couldn't convince the dark men of that. Periodically they would glance up at it fearfully while executing their harsh duties.

The men unloaded crates and stuffed boxes from a flatbed truck, carrying the items to transports, three big trucks—one of which was being worked on by two mechanics. The boxes overflowed with packing materials, making the containers look bloated and sick. As the men traversed back and forth from the truck to the plane, they muttered in their native tongue, looking up at the sun as if it might detach from the heavens and roll over the land like a molten boulder.

The sun seemed to appear closer to the earth than usual. It filled the horizon, lurching above the low, rolling hills and bright green bush like a sniper who'd come too close to his prey.

The hot rays spilled beyond a low brownish green mountain

range and into the thick jungle, landing finally on the cracked ground of the road in Laundi, a small village that wasn't even a speck on the map between the Rwandan border and Kisangani in Central Africa.

United States Secretary of Commerce Donald Howard felt a sense of dread as he stood on the side of the road near the beginnings of the bush. But it wasn't the sun that made him nervous.

What did fill the secretary with dread were the sights he'd seen in the last few weeks, the utter ruin and death he'd witnessed in Southern and Central Africa.

The AIDS virus had devastated the continent in the last two decades. Howard had been sent by the president to survey the condition of the area and determine the size of a package of economic aid.

As an African American, Howard had taken on the assignment with pride and determination. He'd hoped that his trip to the motherland would result in a cultural awakening for him, a long-lost connection to his past. What he found in Africa was quite different: economic mayhem, corruption, intra-African racism, a crumbling infrastructure, and a dispirited people.

And death.

The epidemic had swept the land like a biblical plague, tearing life from the bosom of civilization. Villages were turned into ghost towns, streets were lined with the sick and dying, and rivers were clogged with corpses whose souls had been ripped from their bodies. It was hell on earth, he thought, devastation like none he'd ever witnessed. And for all his authority, he was powerless to help any of these people. A tiny organism had laid waste an entire civilization, and all he could do was watch.

"We're almost ready, sir," said George Gorman. He was one of Howard's Secret Service agents. "The mechanics have pretty much fixed the engine problem in your transport."

Howard was startled for a moment and then looked directly into the eyes of the man who'd just spoken.

Agent Gorman was a tall, lean man of forty or so. He had bright blue eyes and a jaw that was wider than it should have been. It made his head seem a little too big on his shoulders and gave him a look of menace that had served him well in his profession. Gorman was one of two Secret Service men assigned to Howard. Gorman and his partner in turn led a security team comprised of four soldiers, two marines, and two army officers. He stood next to Howard, waiting for him to respond.

"How much longer?" Howard asked impatiently.

"About a half hour, sir," said Gorman.

"Fine," said Howard. "I just want to get out of here as soon as possible. Go and sit on the mechanics."

Gorman nodded and ran off quickly. Howard took a deep breath, letting the strong odors of the land into his lungs. He looked out at the beauty of Africa and was struck by the irony of the wreckage that lay behind it. It was truly a dark continent, he thought.

He didn't like the thought of going to Rwanda by land, but the plane the army had provided for them had malfunctioned. And now the armored truck was down as well. It seemed fate was conspiring to keep him in this desolate area.

Howard would have a compelling story to tell the president, he thought, and he hoped the American government would not hesitate to come to the assistance of these afflicted people. *My people*, he corrected himself, because he had a connection to the citizens here. Howard had seen the faces of his family and friends in the battered visages of this land, and he felt the undeniable nexus of race.

Africa had gotten into his heart. He was linked to this continent by more than skin color. When he first set foot on the ground, he'd felt a rush of emotion flow into him. It was as if he had been here before, as if this trip were his destiny. He didn't believe in past lives, but there was definitely a sense that he was *meant* to be here somehow. He allowed himself to smile a little at the memory.

Suddenly Howard felt a presence at his side and turned to see Alex Deavers standing by him. Alex's silent approach spoke volumes about the man himself. He moved like a cat, quiet and graceful. Alex was of medium build, but muscular and sturdy. He seemed always to be standing at attention, betraying his military background. His dark hair was packed into a neat, modified crew cut. His deep-set eyes were almost black. He was a handsome man, but he seemed to be fighting it, and the last thing you noticed about Alex was the most interesting thing of all: He was not safe. Just behind the handsome face and the easy manner was a personality that would go to the extremes of human behavior at a moment's notice. It was there in his eyes, his lips, the subtle contours of his face. You didn't ever want to push him.

Deavers was the second half of the Secret Service team. He hadn't been with the SS for long, but he came highly recommended. Gorman led the military and coordinated security checks wherever they went, and Deavers stuck closer to Howard as a personal guard. For this reason Howard appreciated Deavers's subtle menace even more.

"Don't worry, sir," said Deavers in a voice that was deceptively soft and mellow. "We'll be out soon."

"I'm basically calm," said Howard, "but you'll excuse me if I seem a little on edge. It's not every day that I witness a holocaust."

"We knew it was bad, sir," said Deavers. "We had all the briefing reports."

"But I wasn't ready for bodies piled to my waist," said Howard, "families dying in one another's arms, men raping young girls because they think sex with a virgin will cure AIDS." He took in a deep breath and then said, "And what happened last night."

"We're not even sure if that's authentic," said Deavers. "I mean, this is Africa, after all."

"You as a white man cannot possibly fathom what that incident might mean," said Howard. Slowly he pulled up a black briefcase that was attached to his wrist by a thick cable and a steel handcuff. He shook it a bit to emphasize his point.

"I'm a citizen of the United States," said Deavers, a little upset. "I know there's something bigger at stake."

"I'm sorry," said Howard, sensing the other man's mood. "I just . . . What do I tell the president about what I know? More to the point, what will he do when he finds out?"

"That would be *his* job," said Deavers. "Yours is to report what you know, and mine is to get you back safely."

Howard nodded slightly, acknowledging the logic of the statement.

"I'll go and make sure Gorman isn't slacking off," Deavers said. "It's his fault that the transport isn't ready."

He excused himself and moved off toward the transports. Howard watched him walk away. Deavers's military gait was even more apparent now.

Deavers was right about the information he carried, Howard thought, but even his reason could not stop the fear he felt this morning.

Two days ago he'd met with General Kiko Salli, a local strongman, one of several who ruled the area. General Salli's father, Nelson, had been a legendary chieftain during the 1930s and '40s. Nelson had worked with several U.S. presidents through three wars and countless calamities, until he'd been overthrown for democratic rule in the 1970s.

Kiko had inherited more than his father's vast fortune when Nelson died. He'd also obtained all of the intelligence that had been gathered over the years, including information on many covert American operations in Africa and Eastern Europe and a curious prize: an official U.S. communiqué naming Lee Harvey Oswald as the suspect in the Kennedy assassination some three hours before President Kennedy had been shot. And then there was the thing that Howard had seen the night before, a piece of information so evil that Howard's hands had shaken when he held it.

"This is my gift to you, my American brother," Salli had said in his melodic voice. "May we all one day be free."

The "gift" had cost Howard fifty thousand dollars.

All great men experienced a moment in time when they could feel destiny tugging at their sleeves. Howard suddenly felt that his moment had come. He saw himself at the center of the biggest story of the new century. He would rise to heights of power he'd never imagined; his name would live in history.

Howard felt himself go calm, felt his heart start to beat in a more normal rhythm and tension seep from his limbs. He *was* great, he thought, and he would show the world soon.

Deavers returned a few moments later, and they walked out toward the big trucks. Howard, Deavers, and his staff of two climbed aboard one. Two of the military men got into the one in front of Howard's transport. Gorman and the other two men got into the last truck. One of Howard's staffers, an ex–army sergeant, drove the truck.

They would drive to Rwanda and then get on the government's regular air force plane and fly back to the coast. Then another larger plane would take Howard back to America.

He settled into his seat next to Deavers. He heard Gorman outside, barking orders to someone. Howard patted his briefcase absently.

"As soon as we get to the city," said Howard, "I want transport to our plane."

"The Rwandan officials will be pissed off," said Deavers. "They wanted to confer with you again before you left."

"They're just making a play for a larger slice of the pie," said Howard. "I'll apologize later."

The trucks began to roll down the bumpy dirt road. After a few moments, Howard felt more of his anxiety slip away. The truck had reinforced, bulletproof side panels, and the men who surrounded him were all trained to protect and kill if necessary.

Howard took off the briefcase's handcuff and rubbed his wrist. He'd had it on all day, and it was starting to hurt. He set the case down.

"Damn thing's a bitch," he said. "Listen, Alex, I wanted to ask you something about what happened last night."

Howard looked over at Deavers, who was preoccupied with something, looking back at the truck behind them.

"Something wrong?" asked Howard.

"They're slowing down," said Deavers. "Falling behind."

"Dammit," said Howard. "That truck is on the fritz, too."

"Then Gorman should call us," said Deavers, "and— Shit! Stop the truck!" Every alarm in his body was going off. He jumped from his seat. "Stop this damned truck! Everybody get off—now!"

The driver braked. Deavers went to the door and opened it as the truck slowed. He saw the black case on the floor in front of the secretary and instinctively grabbed it. He pushed open the door and began to step out as he heard a loud buzz from the floor of the truck. In the next instant, he felt the air around him charge with energy. Then he saw a flash of light as the truck exploded.

Deavers was blown out of the truck. The left side of his face felt hot, then numb, as he was lifted into the air. His body twisted, and then something slammed into his limbs, filling every cell in his body with pain.

In that last moment, Deavers's mind registered the clues he'd missed: the plane's suddenly being unavailable, the mechanical problem with the secretary's transport, the long time it had taken to fix it. All these things should have told him of the plot that had just unfolded.

He was losing his edge, he thought absently. But it was too late for blame, he said to himself. He'd failed. They were all dead, and whoever had paid Gorman to do this had won.

He thought about Kiko Salli and the terrible secret he'd sold to the secretary. His final thought was, It's real.

Unlucky Three

Luther Green held himself perfectly still as the killers entered. They kicked in the flimsy door to the hotel room and rushed in with their silenced Uzi pistols out in front. One of the men lifted his eyes to the ceiling to see whether Luther was there, but all he saw was the sickly yellow water-damaged ceiling. The man lowered his weapon to eye level, and they began to search the room.

Another man rushed to the window, which was slightly ajar, and carefully stuck his head out. He looked left and right to see whether his prey was on the ledge. No one was there.

Luther stood beyond them, silent, motionless. His breathing was thin and measured. He was there but not there, a man but also part of the building. Luther stood just beyond them inside a wall next to an open window. When he'd arrived, he'd spent a lot of time cutting the hole, emptying the wall, and making a door hinge. His electronic eyes, called Tiger Eyes, darted this way and that to spot all of his quarry.

Three of them, he thought. Always a problem when there were

three. When there was a duo, the men tended to stay together, making it easier to get them with groupings of shots. Even if they split apart, they would do so symmetrically, allowing you to hit them with two guns. But three usually meant one would break away from the other two and become a danger to you while you took care of the pair. That had been one of his first lessons in multiple-adversary combat.

His training was always a comfort at times like this. It gave you a foundation, a structure to work from. The mission had a low probability for death, but when you were dealing with these kinds of men, you had to accept that anything could happen.

Luther's mind began to drain itself of the reason and limitation that most people had when it came to violence. The mission, he thought, was paramount, and these men were just obstacles standing in the way of its completion. At this point he knew he would not extricate himself from this situation without violence and fatalities. And yet he could not kill them all.

Luther was in Stockholm to gather information on a group of freelance terrorists. Actually, the group financed terrorism, but according to most governments, that was a distinction without a difference. The group, known to the agency only as Haklim, sold drugs, killed for profit, and conducted elaborate financial scams to fund the operations of their compatriots around the globe. They sold murder and destruction to the highest bidder, and business had been good lately.

The post–September 11 world was always in need of Haklim's many talents. They'd funded the bombing of a Catholic church in South America, killing seven. They'd defrauded German investors out of $3 million for stock in a bogus digital-TV company, and with the proceeds they'd purchased high-tech weapons that

they sold to warring factions in North Africa. Their latest endeavor had been to kill an American businessman who had
bought in to several Kuwaiti oil concerns.

Unfortunately for Haklim, that businessman was really a front
for U.S. government interests. Naturally it did not sit well with
Washington when the man was gunned down.

So Luther had been sent to get the goods on Haklim and bring
them into the light of justice. It was his first "NK," or nonkilling,
mission in three years. The president was putting out many fires
around the world, and he couldn't let one like this go on burning.

Haklim's agents were smart, intuitive men. One of them had
found Luther's little camera mounted in the hotel wall. Luther
had been watching them and recording everything they did and
said when one of them noticed the camera and ripped it from
the wall.

The agents had to know from their own training that the surveillance room must be nearby, and they quickly found Luther's
room one floor up.

The men moved about the room, and Luther's visual-contact
device, or VCD, followed them. It looked like a cheap hotel table
lamp, but encased within its domed black head was a camera with
a 360-degree viewing capacity. Its transmission went directly to his
Tiger Eyes, which looked like normal dark glasses.

Haklim would be quick to find him, so Luther made sure that
all the information he had was saved and stored away while the
agents were bursting into every room on the floor. Then he set
the VCD, put on the sunglasses, and stepped into the wall space,
careful to hide any tracks to it he might have left. He was safe for
the time being, but he had only seconds to surprise them.

The agents chattered in some Arabic dialect, one of the ones

Luther didn't understand. Then, sure enough, a tall man with a shaved head broke away from the other two and walked over to a closet. He pointed his weapon at the closed door and spoke in English:

"We have you, my friend," said the bald man. "Come out." He waited a moment and then fired into the closet. The Uzi popped softly but got a little louder toward the end of the spray. It was hard to silence a pistol so compact and powerful. The bald man opened the door but found no one inside.

Luther felt that it was time. His muscles tightened, and when the men turned, they would begin to search the walls, and he would be found.

Luther took off the Tiger Eyes, pushed open the wall, and swung into the room, pulling out a silenced Namor 48, a new agency weapon that was sleeker and shot faster than the Uzi. The Namor's bullets were about the same size as those of a regular .45, but the casings were made of an aluminum-steel alloy, based on the Agency's old DH-9s, that literally exploded on impact. The Namor was an efficient killer and left ballistics experts little to trace when the corpses were analyzed.

Luther's feet hit the floor in the room, and his first shots got the two men who were grouped together. The Namor coughed hollowly, and a spray of bullets struck them each in the head. The two men twisted, crumpling into each other and falling to the floor.

Before they were eliminated, Luther saw for the first time that one of them was in fact a woman. But even if he had known this, he wouldn't have changed his tactics. Any woman in Haklim would kill just as quickly as a man.

The third man, the unlucky one, had his gun up, but Luther

had already angled to one side and was stooping. The man was caught off balance, and the Uzi pistol had a nasty pull that always left you off target. His shots sailed a good foot over Luther's left shoulder.

Luther had already pulled his other sidearm, a Walther P99, and sent a single shot into the third man's gun hand. It exploded in a misting of red. The Uzi he held dropped to the floor with a clatter. Luther hadn't used the Namor because he needed this man alive.

Luther quickly shot the fallen man and woman again in the head, then went to the third man, who had fallen to his knees. With his good hand, the injured man reached into his pants for something.

Luther ran over to the fallen man and snapped a kick into his ribs, hearing the bones crack wetly. The man grunted hard, his lungs expelling air. Luther grabbed his good arm and wrenched it forward; then, with all his weight, he dropped a knee into the elbow, breaking it. It made another sick sound as the man yelled. Luther hit him hard in the jaw, stopping the noise.

Luther then pulled a cloth from his pocket and stuffed it into the man's mouth, pushing the thick fabric until he felt it going down the man's throat. The man continued to yell in pain.

The Haklim were reported to store poison capsules in their jaws, and Luther didn't want to take the chance that the man would swallow his. He had to take one of them back alive, since he hadn't gotten all the information he needed. This man would have to do.

Luther quickly tied up the man's arms, taking care to put a tourniquet on the bleeding one. The broken arm flopped sadly as he tied it to the bloody one.

He pulled out a hypodermic needle and administered a shot to the man, whose body instantly went completely limp. Luther took the cloth from the man's throat and checked his mouth. His teeth appeared normal, except for one molar that looked unhealthy. It gave way easily. Luther popped the tooth out of his jaw, and sure enough a tiny black capsule was tucked under the fake molar. Luther took out the capsule and popped it into a small plastic bag. The agency would want to analyze it, perhaps make an antidote to the poison for future missions.

Luther stood in the middle of the carnage for a moment. At six-two, his long frame was angular, and even though he was fully clothed, you could see the muscles of his finely toned body. Absently the thought crossed his mind that he was hungry and hadn't eaten since early that morning.

Luther went into the closet and removed the mission case he'd hidden in the back. It was a large black steamer trunk with wheels. He stuffed the third man's unconscious body into it. Then he packed away all their weapons and his VCD. He had to move. The noise of Haklim's searching and the ensuing fight would have attracted attention.

Luther took out a small cell phone, an odd-looking oval thing called an Ion that served many functions. He punched in a series of codes. The phone clicked a few times as it established a link with the agency's secure network.

"Twelve, six," said Luther. His voice was a mildly raspy baritone, a distinctive voice that he had learned to disguise when need be. It sounded rather loud in the silence of the room. He lowered it ever so slightly.

"Status?" said a voice on the radio.

"Seven," said Luther. "Cargo coming. Request cleanup."

"Authorized," said the voice. "Proceed to blue."

Luther turned off the Ion. He took out a gray box from his mission case and opened it. He removed a container and poured a brownish liquid over the two dead men. Then he set their bodies on fire. The flames quickly spread up the walls and across the floor.

Luther wheeled his hidden captive out of the hotel as fire alarms sounded and the building was evacuated. People rushed around him as he calmly and quickly rolled his cargo from the building.

Black smoke wafted into the bright morning sky as Luther pushed the suitcase holding the third man to his truck. Mentally he chastised himself for the mistakes he'd made. He had obviously not hidden his camera well enough. Even his cleanup had been sloppy, although the compound he poured on the dead men would reduce their bodies to ashes, making them incapable of being identified. He'd made mistakes, but he hadn't been exposed, and his duty would be discharged.

Luther moved toward what looked to be an American family on vacation. The commotion had gotten their attention, and they were walking toward the hotel. The father was a portly man of about forty or so, accompanied by a soccer-mom wife and two towheaded kids of about ten or so. Luther walked closer to them and was surprised when the father looked at him and spoke.

"Excuse me. Do you know what's going on?" he asked excitedly.

"J'ai entendu qu'un incendie s'est déclaré au premier étage!" said Luther excitedly in French.

"Oh, I'm sorry," said the father in that loud way Americans

have when they find out that everyone in the world doesn't speak English. "Sorry."

Luther nodded stupidly, and the family moved on. Luther smiled and continued on his own way. He was a half mile down the road when there was an explosion in the hotel, completing his mission.

Hampton

Luther drove quickly through the streets of the city, thinking about the dying man in his trunk. He did not want to drive recklessly and be stopped by the locals, so he was careful to obey any posted limits.

Stockholm was a beautiful place, filled with historic sites and architectural wonders. He drove his Mercedes through a thriving marketplace close to Hammarby Sjöstad, the city's largest housing project. Stockholm had many government-funded housing projects, and unlike the ones in the United States, they were sought-after places of style and comfort.

Luther rounded a corner and headed toward Natasha's, a local eatery that fronted for the agency and served as its sector safe house.

He pulled his vehicle to the back of the place, cursing under his breath as he slowed to a crawl in the alley. The streets and passageways in Europe were so damned narrow. And of course the agency would have given him an SUV to drive on this mission.

Luther got out and wheeled his cargo past some men unloading a food truck. He quickly headed for the bowels of the basement. When he got down there, Luther faced a dark brick wall with an old wooden door. He pulled out the Ion and hit a button, and a thin shaft of red light erupted from the end. Luther scanned that wall with the laser until it found a matching laser source in a brick about a foot over his head. The light sources met, and something behind the wooden door hummed. Luther stood back as it opened, revealing the CIA's safe house.

The Agency doctors and med techs took the prisoner and administered emergency procedures. They set the broken arm and began to work on the shattered, bleeding hand.

"You guys are so damned messy," said a doctor to Luther.

"He's alive," said Luther. "Keep him that way." Even he could hear the tense tone of his voice. The doctor regarded Luther briefly then and started to work faster.

Behind the dark wall, the safe house was clean, bright, and sterile. When agents came, you never knew whether they would walk in with a shopping bag and a smile or with a bleeding, dying hostage. The staff was prepared for anything.

The hallway was wide and long; the walls and floor were white and plain. A security camera was posted in a corner at the end of the hallway by an inner entrance.

"How much did you give him?" the doctor asked Luther.

"Only ten cc's," he responded.

"Good. There won't be a danger of cardiac arrest," said the doctor, almost to himself.

Luther stood back as a gurney was brought out and the prisoner was placed on it and whisked away.

"You're on the local news," said a voice through a speaker near the camera.

"Couldn't be avoided," said Luther. "I caught a seven."

"Sloppy," said the voice. "I'd never let that happen to me."

"That's because the hard work is left to the professionals."

"Come on in, Luther," said the voice. "I'll buy you a drink. You're gonna need it."

Marcellus Hampton was an extremely unassuming man. He was thirty years old, stood five foot eight inches tall, and had dark brown hair and a face with features that were neither handsome nor homely. He was the kind of guy who blended in anywhere he went. He might be an American, a European, an aristocrat, or white trash.

But Hampton's eyes told a different story. They possessed an energy that said there was more to this ordinary-looking man than one might think. Hampton was a certified genius. He had enrolled in college at age twelve, had graduated with an advanced degree from MIT at fourteen and after that from the prestigious and very secret government technology school in Maine, Seacrest Academy.

Hampton amazed all his teachers as he went beyond their every expectation. His parents were at first shocked and then happy when he proved exceptional, especially his father, a lifetime military man. Their happiness ended when it was apparent that the government was going to take custody of their genius son. They made peace with it once the checks started to arrive monthly. Hush money. And it was better than going to sleep and waking up in a security facility.

After Hampton completed Seacrest, he decided to work for the CIA, turning down NASA, the FBI, the NSA, and the Orion Think Tank in London. Hampton loved technology and information, and when the Agency called, he was very eager to go, since the CIA was known to be in the forefront of all technological advances. He was there only a year before he was recruited into E-1, the ultrasecret agency that employed both him and Luther Green.

Hampton was a TWA, or tech and weapons adviser. He helped an agent coordinate and plan his mission and worked as a field assistant and backup if needed. Luther had worked with many TWAs, but Hampton was the best. They'd been working together for five years now and had become good friends.

Hampton poured Luther a glass of sweet brandy in his office. It was a spacious room, not unlike those occupied by big-time CEOs. The office had nice furnishings, but none of them belonged to Hampton. He was a tenant in this place. The only things he'd brought were pictures of his parents and his current girlfriend, a willowy blonde who stood an inch taller than he.

"Anything I should know about this one?" asked Hampton.

"It'll all be in my report," said Luther. "The one I brought in should know something that will help us crack the Haklim."

"So how did you blow your cover?" asked Hampton.

"They found my camera in the wall. I didn't hide it well enough. Tell me why I need this," said Luther, referring to the drink.

"Director Gray called," said Hampton. "We're needed back in the U.S."

Kilmer Gray was the director of E-1. He was one of the most

important men in government, and if he wanted to see you, it was always urgent.

"Any idea why?" Luther was curious. He took a sip of his drink.

"No," said Hampton. "You know the director's motto: Secrets live—"

"Or people die," Luther finished.

"I do know that the agency's computer system has been siphoning a lot of information from domestic police organizations here and abroad in the last month or so, but anyone could find that out," said Hampton.

Luther felt a familiar sense of frustration. It was not uncommon to be summoned for duty, but information was always scarce in the agency, and each assignment seemed to come by ambush. No matter how he tried, he could not get used to this.

"Director Gray wants you back ASAP," said Hampton. "I have to stay here and get whatever information I can from your captive today. I'll follow as soon as I'm done. All your papers and travel plans are ready. You leave tomorrow, traveling under the name Tennison."

Luther said good-bye to his friend and left for his quarters. He moved through the quiet hallways, listening to the click of his own footfalls on the floor. The muffled music from Natasha's was distant above him. That was the life of an agent, he thought, just inches away from real life.

Luther walked into his suite, a well-appointed and very comfortable room. He ate some leftovers from a minifridge, then got into bed and settled in. He opened his suitcase and took out his collection of CDs. Luther's musical tastes were eclectic. Music should be pure, he thought, and that kind of music was rare nowadays.

Luther's music collection was divided into two sections. He flipped past the rap section, passing Cee-Lo, Nas, and a Tribe Called Quest and moving to the classical section. He took out *Favourite Piano Sonatas by Vladimir Ashkenazy* and put it in the room's CD player. Soon the soothing sounds of Beethoven's Adagio sostenuto in C-sharp filled the room.

There was a correlation between rap and the classics, he believed. Not in style but passion. The masters' music was filled with strong emotion, as was the best of hip-hop. But he never listened to rap after a mission. That was premission music. After his having risked his life, only the classics could lull him to sleep and allow him to forget the dark side of his occupation.

Luther closed his eyes and let the music move through him. What kind of world could produce such beauty as Beethoven and the horror that was the Haklim? And what kind of man was he? He'd killed two of them, severely wounded another, and settled in for the night as if he'd just had a pizza, some beer and bowled ten frames.

But this was the way of E-1. The disciplines of the agency made you a killer but told you that you were upholding the law. This ran the risk that agents might come to believe they were above the laws they upheld. This is why the agency made philosophy part of its order. Eventually this philosophy led to a set of rules that governed agents on a mission. The E-1 rules, all 224 of them, covered every aspect of mission behavior. But they were as much moral code as procedure. They taught an agent to take life, but only in the protection of freedom, and to respect that this power was derived from the will of greater authority.

Luther relaxed and tried to let go of the many disturbing thoughts in his head. His mission in Sweden was finished, and now, like any good agent, he was thinking forward to the next. Part of him wanted to go out into the city and have a little fun. The Swedes loved to party, and he admitted that he was missing female companionship these days. Even Beethoven couldn't make up for that.

He let go of this desire and stayed in bed as the next track started to play. He'd let Ludwig put him to sleep, and he'd leave the dangers of tomorrow for tomorrow.

Secret's Shadow

Luther drove to the E-1 home base just outside Washington, D.C. He had not been there in about two years, and he wondered whether it would feel strange going back.

E-1 undertook all of the dangerous, covert, and illegal missions the government needed carried out in foreign lands. If a foreign threat had reached American shores, E-1 might be called upon, but this was unusual. They were the "spooks," the nameless, faceless government men who did the secret biddings that later became curious headlines and urban legends.

E-1 was not affiliated with the CIA but did share some common history. It's funding was secret, although some speculated that some of the bloat in federal budgets found its way into E-1 coffers. Still other stories told of the agency's taking money from very bad men and putting it to better use. All Luther knew was that his generous salary was wire-transferred into his account each month, and the agency took care of all his living needs.

The agency had no ties to any official governmental unit, so the president and Congress would always have plausible deniability of any actions taken. In short, E-1 did not exist.

The department had been started almost by accident. During World War II, as Hitler's threat swept the world, President Roosevelt became concerned about the dictator's malevolent global influence. Roosevelt was worried that Hitler would succeed in his conquest of Europe and, along with the Russians, challenge U.S. authority after the war.

So FDR called together the greatest minds from the scientific, military, and political communities and put them in a group he called Horizon. It was housed in the same building as the Office of Strategic Services, the OSS.

Horizon's job was to determine how big a threat Hitler was and what the United States should do about it. In the end the answer was simple: Hitler had to die. Roosevelt and later Truman would commission an elite team of assassins to do the job. They were pulled from the army's, the navy's, and the marines' elite service units and trained in Canada for more than a year in intelligence gathering, covert operations, and methods of elimination. They were called the Elite Corps.

The EC did not kill Hitler, but several of his generals and other key players in the Nazi Party were quietly dispatched during the war. Domestically the Elite Corps eliminated several double agents and averted a planned assassination of Harry Truman.

The OSS was the precursor to the CIA, which was formally created in 1947 with the signing of the National Security Act by President Truman. "Give 'Em Hell Harry" wasn't pleased with the idea that a foreign government would try to have him bumped off, so he took measures to make sure it would never happen again.

The National Security Act charged the director of Central Intelligence with coordinating the nation's spy activities and correlating, evaluating, and disseminating information that affected national security.

The Elite Corps was eventually disbanded by Truman—or at least that was the official word. Unofficially the EC was kept funded to assist the nation in eliminating its enemies. During the Cold War, the EC team was called to action in the fight against the Red Menace. It was then that it was renamed E-1, had the fact of its existence erased from all official documents, and was given the power to kill anyone America considered a threat. There was some debate about the wisdom of this, but in the end communism was thought to pose a bigger danger than did a band of patriotic killers.

E-1 was briefly suspended when Kennedy was assassinated. But the agency was eventually cleared of any involvement, and its work continued. E-1 has existed quietly since then through many presidential administrations, wars, and conflicts. There is a joke in government that the president knows he has killers at his disposal but doesn't know who they are. If the government has secrets, then E-1 is the shadow of those secrets.

E-1 was housed in a plain-looking building at 15 Standard Avenue, not too far from CIA headquarters in Langley. The windowless white structure looked more like a warehouse than an office building. E-1 shared space with the Veterans Administration, and several floors were given to the Social Security Administration. But E-1 had most of the building undercover as a special arm of the General Accounting Office. There were in fact people there who did accounting for the GAO, but E-1's main activities had nothing to do with balance sheets. Everyone who worked in the building had a high security-clearance level, un-usual for a nonpolicing authority, but no one in the VA or SSA asked any questions about it. In federal civil service, it didn't pay to get too nosy.

Luther entered the building and headed toward the back, where a wall hid a bank of elevators from the view of anyone in the main lobby. He walked up to the two big guards and flashed his ID. They ran a scanner over it and moved to let him onto the elevator. The car went down one floor to the first base-ment.

Luther got out of the car and walked to the reception area. The room looked innocent enough, like any business lobby, but if there was a security "situation," the room would lock the one door and the back entrance to the main facility, turning it into a little prison cell.

In the middle of the small lobby, at a dark mahogany desk, sat a sour-faced woman in her fifties. She did not look up as Luther walked up to her.

"Good morning, Adelaide," said Luther. "Nice to see you again."

Adelaide raised her head, and Luther could see that she was hunched over a small computer. Her pale blue eyes appeared large behind her glasses. "Back already?" she asked. "I thought we were rid of you, Green."

"I've been gone for two years." Luther smiled down at her.

"Seems like yesterday to me. I guess I'm getting older. Time gets shorter, and then one day it stops, because you're dead."

"Why are you stalling?" he asked Adelaide.

"Smart boy," she said. "We're doing longer security checks. We had a little terrorist trouble in New York. Maybe you heard about it while you were over there in that country with the free dope and hookers."

"It's not free. It's just legal, and I wasn't in *that* country," said Luther.

Adelaide Gibson had been one of their best field agents in the seventies. Back then she was a stunning beauty, a brunette with long legs and an infectious smile.

Her story was legend in E-1. Adelaide had been on assignment in Africa when the warring nations were causing a potential imbalance in the Cold War. Both the communist powers and the United States were trying to sway African nations their way, or at best keep them fighting so that their influence was nugatory.

Adelaide's husband, Mark, was a regular CIA agent who'd been sent to Africa a year before on a special assignment. When Adelaide got there, she found he had been corrupted by a communist-backed regime. Mark asked her to join him in taking the money and looking the other way, and she agreed, just long enough to turn him in, along with the entire group.

Adelaide's husband was convicted of treason and several other crimes. Mark Gibson couldn't live with the ruin of his life, so he committed suicide in prison. Adelaide had stood by him during his ordeal, but after he died, she quietly had a nervous breakdown and then retired from field duty. Now she sat at a desk, made a decent salary, and worked the controls of the second security station at E-1.

"So there's been whispering about you," she said. "I hope it's good."

"Me, too," said Luther.

"Outer doors secure. Inner online," said Adelaide. "Three seconds."

The doors at the rear of the lobby opened. Luther said good-bye to Adelaide and walked through.

Inside Security Station Two, Luther was faced with a large metal detector and guards dressed in the classic bland dark suits. Luther stood behind a glass wall made of thick, attack-proof glass and waited.

He said hello to everyone, and he could see that Adelaide was right. They'd all obviously been talking about him. They had that look in their eyes that something was being hidden.

Luther took out his sidearm, the Walther P99, and placed it in the gun chute. All E-1 agents chose their own sidearms. He liked the P99 because of its lightweight polymer frame and the recoil compensator that steadied it when he fired. It was much like an agent, an efficient killer.

Luther stood in front of a small scanner and placed his hand on it. The machine scanned his hand- and fingerprints.

"Come on in, Agent Green," said one of the guards. "Welcome back, sir."

The security door opened, and Luther went inside. He retrieved his P99 and then moved down the hallway to a bank of elevators. He got on one of them and pressed the button for level six. The elevator went down. In any other agency, the boss would reside on the top floor, not the lowest one. Luther often wondered what it meant that the agency liked to house itself underground. He knew that this structure had a reinforced skeleton that acted as a second roof. If the building toppled, you could survive for weeks under the wreckage.

Luther got off on level six, which they called "Deep Six," and headed for the director's office. He passed through double glass doors into E-1's operations room. It was a busy bullpen, with state-of-the-art informational equipment.

The twenty or so workers here all kept track of the fifty-three E-1 agents all around the globe. Luther scanned the big world map on the far wall and saw the glittery gold buttons that represented the agents. A button locked in to his exact position in Virginia. That was him, he thought, reduced to a little golden speck.

Luther was greeted by Thomas, a thin man of about thirty. He was Kilmer Gray's personal assistant, and if you left it to him, he would tell you that he was running the shop.

"Luther, you're right on time," said Thomas happily. "Director Gray is just finishing up."

"Good. Thank you, Thomas," said Luther.

Luther tried not to frown. He didn't make small talk with Thomas. Luther didn't like to hear him go on and on about his closeness to his powerful boss, so he just smiled and sat down. Thomas was a pain, although he was known to be quite proficient in several areas of training.

Thomas looked at him a little too long, and Luther felt that sense again that he'd been discussed before his arrival. Thomas smiled, trying to cover his obvious expression, and then walked away to his station.

Luther sat in the plush leather chair against the wall and waited. He didn't have to wait long. Director Gray's office door opened, and just then on the map, two agents' gold specks sprouted red lines that stopped in Jerusalem.

Kilmer Gray ambled out of his office. He was a smallish man who tended to stoop at the shoulders. He had a tangle of salt-and-pepper hair and sharp dark eyes under lids that always seemed half closed.

Kilmer surveyed the situation room, and to Luther he looked like a hawk surveying his domain. His face was stony and expressionless, the face of a man who never wanted you to know what he was thinking. He turned slightly, making sure the agents had been relocated on the map. Then his eyes came to rest on Luther.

Kilmer's expression didn't change. He walked over to Luther, extending his hand. "Luther. Good to see you."

"You, too, sir," said Luther.

Luther stood, and the two men shook hands. Kilmer's was cool, and this had always bothered Luther for some reason. His grip was firm, but it was an icy thing, and Luther was always a little happier when Kilmer released him. The men walked into Kilmer's office.

Director Gray's office was an expansive place filled with ornate furniture made of rich wood. The walls were covered with paintings done by the director himself. Lighthouses and dark cottages were his favorite subjects. Luther had forgotten that Kilmer was so talented. You might have thought you were in a professor's study until you saw that on the wall behind his long desk was a smaller version of the map in the situation room.

Kilmer Gray had been in government service all his adult life. He was drafted out of West Point and shocked his family by joining the Green Berets. He served with distinction in Vietnam, accumulating quite a kill record. Kilmer left the service and joined the FBI briefly but soon reenlisted in the army and advanced to the rank of general.

He proved to be a ruthless adversary, and his intellect helped the country win many a day overseas. When a suicide bomber killed a batch of marines, it was Kilmer who planned the counterresponse that brought about the deaths of fifty suspected enemies over the next two years. The operation was methodical, flawless, and untraceable. It wasn't long before the bureaucrats came calling, and Kilmer was sent into the CIA. He served in various capacities, including as Director of Intelligence. When he was asked to become the head of E-1, he accepted the assignment without hesitation.

Kilmer had never married, and although he'd kept company with many women over the years, he led a solitary life. The job was his woman, people said behind his back, and it was true. Kilmer Gray was married to E-1, and it was for better or worse and until death.

"You'll be happy to know that the Haklim agent you captured in Stockholm gave us vital information," said Kilmer, sitting down and motioning Luther to do the same. "Mr. Hampton is quite efficient in using drugs to extract information."

"Yes, he is good," said Luther, sitting.

Luther didn't ask what the information was, nor did he inquire about what had become of the third man. It was not his job to know such things. He'd completed his mission, and that was all he'd been paid to do. But he couldn't help thinking that the Haklim agent had been drained of all useful information and then shipped off to the holding facility in the Philippines, where he would eventually be eliminated cleanly.

"Alex Deavers is alive," said Kilmer flatly.

Luther was shocked. He straightened in his chair and did his best to play down his emotions. Kilmer was not one to mince words, and he relished getting to the point. If Luther knew Kilmer, the fact that Alex was alive was just the first part of the matter.

Alex Deavers had brought Luther into E-1, had trained him and eventually become one of his best friends. When Alex was reported to be dead, Luther had taken the news hard. But that was the life, he'd told himself. He was prepared at any time for the death of any of the men and women he knew in the business. Still, he had never worried much about Alex. He was one of the agency's best operatives and had cheated death many times. Apparently he'd done it at least once more.

"Where is he?" asked Luther in a measured tone.

"That's part of why you're here. I want you to go after the wolf. Will you?" "Wolf" was the agency term for a rogue agent.

"Yes, sir," said Luther. He did not hesitate. If Kilmer sensed any reluctance, he'd refuse to give him the assignment. Kilmer had obviously thought about the fact that Luther and Alex had a close relationship and the duality it created. Luther was emotionally invested, but he also knew the man well and would be good at anticipating Alex's moves.

Kilmer pushed a button on the lip of his desk, and a two-sided flat-panel monitor popped up. The monitor showed the mission file.

" 'Alex Deavers, E-1 agent, was blown from the transport of the now-deceased secretary of commerce, Donald Howard, on February fifteenth,' " Kilmer began reading. The official story was that the secretary was killed by terrorist sympathizers and that everyone involved had died. "Deavers's cover had been established six months before with the Secret Service. Another Secret Service agent named Gorman was unaccounted for that day," Kilmer continued. "We had first believed that Gorman was dead. But we were mistaken. We then assumed that Gorman was paid to assassinate the secretary. Deavers beat us to that assumption and landed in Germany. He found Gorman in a private home, then tortured and killed him. We got a security photo of Deavers from a train station in Berlin."

"Did he get information from Gorman?" asked Luther.

"Again, presumably," said Kilmer.

"So whatever Gorman knew, we'll never know," said Luther.

"Yes. Deavers is now in possession of that information, too," said Kilmer. Then his brow furrowed, just for a second but long enough for Luther to take notice. His eyes opened a little wider and then returned to their usual half-closed position. "From there he made it to London, where he contacted and killed MI6 agent Lisa Radcliff."

"Lisa," said Luther under his breath.

"Yes, I believe you knew her."

"Alex introduced us, many years ago when I was just starting."

"He contacted her, and then we assume he asked for her assistance. Presumably when it was refused, he resorted to his training."

Luther envisioned a battle between the two agents. Lisa and Deavers had been lovers at one point. No good agent would have been caught off guard, he thought. Lisa was a black belt in tae kwon do. He saw Alex disabling her formidable style and crushing her with his greater power.

"He snapped her neck, in case you're wondering," said Kilmer. "And she put up a fight. His blood was found in her flat. Following this little incident, British authorities came after him. Deavers easily eluded them. One man was killed and two others hospitalized. He killed an agent named Victor Jansen with a mini–stress charge that blew off the man's foot. We believe that it was an item from Radcliff's utility pack."

This was Kilmer's clinical name for what E-1 agents called a "goodie box," an arsenal of weaponry.

"The other two men were beaten badly," Kilmer continued. "We believed that Deavers bribed his way onto a freighter that went into Canada, or at least that *was* what we thought. When we caught up with the man on the ship, he turned out to be an illegal immigrant from Norway."

Kilmer turned off the display panel and then added, "I'm almost proud of him."

"So where do we think he might be?" asked Luther.

"That's where you begin," said Kilmer. "We lost him. He left no ordinarily readable trail—nothing."

"And 'nothing' means an agent is on the case," said Luther, remembering something that Alex had taught him. In the normal discharge of life, people leave evidence that they've been present in a place. There's no reason for a normal person to cover his tracks or otherwise obfuscate the fact of his presence. But the only trail an agent leaves is no trail at all. When it's examined closely by another agent, though, there's always something there.

"This mission is nonrecourse," said Kilmer. His eyelids seemed to close all the way for a moment.

"Why?" asked Luther. He had been thinking that Deavers was to be captured. But for a kill mission, he didn't mind asking Kilmer this.

The director was smart enough not to tell Luther it was a kill mission until he'd given him some information on what his old friend had done. Kilmer would not think of his question as weakness or hesitation. It was a request for more information.

"Deavers is clearly a loose cannon," said Kilmer. "If he was injured in the explosion, he might be mentally imbalanced. We don't know what he's planning, but it can't be good. We can assume that when you catch up to him, he will try to eliminate you just as he has every other agent he's encountered. I will not send an agent after him without teeth in his orders. So do you accept the terms?"

Luther took just a moment, but in that instant he relived his history with Alex, an exceptional man who had introduced Luther to the world and his role in it. Alex was a friend, but Luther was a creature of duty. E-1 was not unlike a sports team, a place where personal achievement never outweighs a common cause. The goal of the team was to win at all costs, and in that regard Luther had no choice.

"Yes, sir," said Luther. "I do."

"You start today," said Kilmer.

"I need to know what Alex was in Africa for."

"He was protecting the secretary and making sure the country's covert positions were being held. The secretary didn't know anything about that."

Luther waited a second for Kilmer to keep talking. When he didn't, he asked, "And his E-1 assignment . . . ?"

Kilmer's look didn't waver, and neither did Luther's. Luther had as much as said to the director that he knew he was holding back vital information. Operatives always had multiple assignments. They received their cover, their stated assignment, and beneath it all there was usually a task specifically for E-1 that came from the director himself.

Kilmer looked at Luther with the blank stare of a man who'd been raised in the agency. It was a look that told nothing but spoke volumes to Luther, who knew Kilmer was measuring his response and the value of the information. Then Kilmer did something Luther wouldn't have thought possible—he laughed.

"If you hadn't asked me, I'd 've thought I'd selected the wrong agent," said Kilmer.

Kilmer went back to the screen and hit a button on his desk. The screen flashed E-1 MISSION FILE: DIRECTOR'S EYES ONLY. The file appeared, showing a picture of an African military man.

"Alex's E-1 mission was to eliminate this man, Supreme Commander Ngamu Behiddah of the Congo region. Behiddah was planning a coup and was allied with several other strongmen known to be hostile to the U.S."

"Behiddah was also rumored to be a terrorist sympathizer," Luther added. "But he was killed by one of his own men, I thought."

"Deavers is an expert in elimination," said Kilmer. He smiled ever so slightly.

Luther admitted being a little jealous. He had checked that story when he saw it, thinking it was an agency hit. But there were no telltale signs of E-1 on it. All the evidence pointed to Behiddah's subcommander as the killer.

"So I assume it wasn't Behiddah's people who paid Gorman," said Luther.

"No. After Alex's elimination of Behiddah, all Behiddah's men were rounded up and killed by his successor." Kilmer looked at Luther with his unreadable stare again, but this time Luther knew what he was thinking.

"Was Alex clean?" Luther asked. "Did we try to backwash him?"

"Backwash" was a field term for the elimination of an assassin after he's completed his mission, in order to clean or "backwash" any witnesses. This was done when an agent was dirty and the agency was onto him.

"No," said Kilmer. "I think Alex might be insane, and right now he may believe that we tried to kill him. Under this delusion he might be allying with our enemies."

"You think he's a traitor?" asked Luther.

"I think he's sick and extremely dangerous," said Kilmer, looking gravely serious. "There are a lot of secrets in that head of his. We need to keep them there by eliminating him. Good luck."

Luther said good-bye, stood, and left the director's office. When he stepped outside, he was immediately met by Thomas, who had an envelope in his hands.

"This is the file and your instructions," Thomas said, handing the thick packet to Luther. "Mr. Hampton is your tech and weapons adviser as usual, and the director will expect contact at all key junctures by the usual channels."

"Thanks," said Luther.

Luther took a few steps and then almost bumped into Frank Hedgispeth, a fellow E-1 agent. Frank was a good agent, but he and Luther had never had an easy relationship. Frank stuck close to home when he could and worked the system for advancement, while Luther did fieldwork. They'd been rivals throughout training, and they'd probably be rivals for power within the agency one day.

"Hey, Luth," said Frank. Luther hated being called "Luth." It was an asinine nickname, but that was Frank's way, always too damned friendly.

"Hey, Hedge," said Luther, remembering Frank's E-1 academy name.

"Back in the old U.S., huh?" said Frank.

"Yes, good to be back."

Thomas had been standing nearby through all of this. Luther shot him a glare, and Thomas scampered off to his desk.

Luther turned back to Frank, who was looking cocky and smug as usual. Luther was sure that Frank wanted to brag to him about something.

"So what you been up to?" asked Luther.

"Nothing much," said Frank. "Hey, did you hear about the Terrorism Task Force in South America? It was coordinated to foster U.S. antiterrorist policies. Some radical political leader opposed it, but he died a month before."

Luther knew in an instant that Frank had headed up that effort and taken out the leader. An agent didn't speak directly of his prior missions. He talked about them as if they were news stories.

Frank's father was a congressman from New York, an ex-military and ex-FBI agent, and his mother was, of all things, an ex-marine. They'd gotten rich working for military suppliers after retiring from the service. They'd brought young Frank into the fold as a full-fledged government blueblood.

"Great. Well, I gotta go. Nice seeing you, Frank."

"Listen, there are three of us here now. Let's go out and have some fun."

Luther glanced at the big map and saw the three gold buttons in Virginia.

"Who's the third?" asked Luther.

"Bane," said Frank, and then he smiled knowingly.

"I'll take you up on that," said Luther. He really didn't want to hang out with Frank, but he did like Sharon Bane, and he hadn't seen her in ages. "Where are we meeting?"

"X Club," said Frank.

"It's a meat market."

"Well, I'm feeling carnivorous today," said Frank.

Luther smiled and walked out of the director's office. He felt Frank bore holes in his back as he did. He moved into the elevator lobby. There was something on his mind as he got into an elevator and made his way out of E-1. The thought stayed with him as he went through an exit security check. Kilmer wanted to make sure you were the same person leaving as you were when you came in.

Luther walked into the bright sunshine as the nagging notion pulled itself out of that pool of doubt that lay beyond his loyalty to his superiors. He'd kept this feeling at bay while he was talking to Kilmer and the others at E-1. Agents were too adept at reading people, and what he was thinking was dangerous at this juncture of the mission.

Information, he said to himself.

Kilmer had said that Deavers had executed his E-1 assignment, killed the target, and later killed Gorman and escaped *"in possession of that information, too."* Then Kilmer's brow had furrowed and his eyes had widened as if he'd made a mistake saying the sentence. The word "too" suggested that there was *additional* information in Alex's possession. If that were true, why hadn't Kilmer said anything about it? Was it information from Deavers's E-1 assignment? Was it just a poor use of words?

These were troubling questions, thought Luther, as troubling as the prospect of killing Alex Deavers.

The Hookup

Luther got into his car and drove away from the facility. It was a mild spring day, and he couldn't remember seeing a more beautiful one. When summer set in, it would get hot and sticky in the D.C. area, and he'd want to be anywhere but here.

Luther didn't head straight home. He went to a nearby mall, where he did some light shopping. He delighted some kids in an arcade while playing a shooting game called House of 1,000 Corpses, where he used two guns to blast zombies to bits. His score had been almost perfect through three levels. When the kids asked what he did for a living, he'd said, "I'm a kind of a cop."

Luther took in a movie and then had dinner at a sit-down restaurant later, where he flirted with a waitress who gave him her cell-phone number. When he got home, it was going on nine o'clock.

The E-1 condo was a modest place just outside the capital. It was a secure building owned by a retired agent who did daily security sweeps. Luther examined his doorjamb and found his polycord seal still intact. Polycord was a transparent spray that hardened into a sealant after application. If anyone had been inside without his permission, the seal would have been broken.

Luther put his electronic key in the lock and heard the series of clicks on the other side, signaling that the computerized security system was disabling itself. He went in, took a quick nap, and then started to get dressed. He put on a hard-driving tune by Tupac. He'd have to listen to whatever crap they played at the X Club, so he'd listen to some good music beforehand.

Luther got dressed in jeans and a black mock turtle that showed off his physique. He glanced at himself in the full-length mirror in his bedroom and was pleased with what he saw. Luther struggled with his handsomeness. It was a good thing at times, but in his heart he felt that too much investment in it might lead to pride, and that was a weakness, something that could be exploited by counteroperatives. A man could be made weak if the right woman came along and the man's belief that he was entitled to her only added to his proclivity to wander away from his obligations.

He put on his leather jacket and was about to go when he was hit by the feeling that he shouldn't. Whenever he was on a mission, he wanted to deprive himself of everything pleasurable, diverting all desire to the intent to succeed. Going out to a club to engage in the sexual rituals of the day seemed like an unnecessary digression. He had to find Alex Deavers, and that was all he would let himself think about.

Luther suppressed this feeling. It was simply a part of the mission mentality, he told himself. In fact, he would have been spooked if he didn't feel this way. He always worked things through in the beginning.

Luther walked out of his condo and engaged the security system. If breached, it would sound an alarm for building security and a corresponding one at E-1, where a strike team would be dispatched to his place. He'd be notified as well. He resealed the door with a layer of polycord and set out.

The X Club was alive with music, bodies, and one-night dreams. The women were beautiful and scantily clad. Luther was again reminded that he hadn't been with a woman in a while, and the admiring stares were getting to him. He ignored the ones from the men.

It was difficult for him to let go of his training in such a place. Even with all the stimuli, he saw things that others might have missed. Two of the waitresses were making drug deals. There were eight bouncers in the place, but only one of them would be trouble to kill. The others he could dispose of in less than five minutes with the proper weapon. In fact, with all the noise and distractions, he could probably kill a couple of people before anyone caught on.

Luther didn't see Sharon Bane or Frank anywhere, so he copped a seat at the bar and waited. He ordered a Rémy martini. The bartender, a beefy white kid with long hair, made a fine one.

Luther caught the scent of perfume coming from his left side. It was subtle and wafted just under the other smells of the place. He could feel her now behind him, moving closer, deliberate in her approach. He was excited, but he didn't turn. That was the first mistake men made with women, giving them too much attention, making them feel that they, the men, were not the ones in control. Even though it could put one's life in danger, the rules of the predator nonetheless applied.

He waited.

"Can I squeeze in?" asked a woman's voice very close to his ear.

Luther didn't say anything. He just shifted his weight and got off his barstool, sliding his drink over. The woman slid in next to him, smiled, and cocked her head to see his face better.

She was pretty and obviously a mixture of several ethnicities— most notably Asian, which was strong in her almond-shaped eyes. She wore a little leather skirt whose top stopped just below her belly, showing off her muscular stomach, which she was undoubtedly very proud of. The swell of her chest caught his eyes, and her dark hair was cut short and feathered nicely.

She was a stunner, he thought, but his face betrayed none of that sentiment. A beautiful woman doesn't want a man she thinks is easy or eager. She wants what she shouldn't have.

If a woman goes through all the bother of getting dressed in sexy attire, fixing her hair, and spending God knows how much on all this, she is not going to hook up with some man who she thinks just wants to put his dick in her and disappear. She wants something more, something special, and if she can't get it, she'll go home alone with her fantasy.

"Thanks," she said.

"No problem," said Luther. He looked at her and didn't stop. He stared directly into her eyes and dropped all pretext from his mind. She saw this, and curiosity started to rise in her face. Luther then turned away, just enough to break the connection.

"Do I know you?" she asked.

He waited a beat, then another, just long enough for her curiosity to peak again. Then he said, "I'm the man you came here to meet tonight."

"Really?" she asked. "Never heard that one before."

She was about to say something else when Luther took her

hand and led her to the dance floor. She followed him with an amused look on her face.

"I don't suppose it would make sense to resist," she said.

"It would," said Luther, "but where's the fun in that?"

They embraced and moved with each other. The song, a bumping, forgettable hip-hop tune, was five times faster than the tempo they were dancing, but they took no notice. Luther was excited and didn't even try to stop the erection building in his pants. He pulled her close to him and felt her hands exploring.

"I'm Tomiko," she whispered.

"Jordan," said Luther. It was the name of a good friend he'd gone to school with.

"Black and Korean, if you're wondering."

"I wasn't, but it's nice to know." Luther said this to her in Korean.

"Oh! You speak it?" she said, surprised. "I'm not so good. What did you say?"

"That it was nice to know."

"You are surprising," said Tomiko. "What kind of black man speaks Korean?"

"Just me," he said, smiling.

Tomiko looked at him for a moment, seemingly unable to respond to his statement. For a while, they merely felt each other's embrace, and Luther could sense that she got his meaning.

"You don't seem like the kind of guy who would come here alone. Where are your friends?"

"They're late," said Luther. "You?"

"My cousin and her friends invited me here on my layover."

They stopped dancing and went back to the bar. It was full, and so they just stood by it, leaning on a bare corner. They talked for twenty minutes or so about nothing. She asked Luther about him-self, and he cleverly avoided telling her anything.

Luther was preparing to start a line of conversation designed to get Tomiko to go to bed with him when he spotted Frank on the other side of the room. Frank saw him, waved, and started to wade through the crowd.

"There's my friend," said Luther.

"It's okay," said Tomiko. "My people got here while we were dancing. I gave them the 'I'm with someone promising' sign."

Luther smiled dutifully, but in truth he had seen her give that sign, a cute little gesture whereby she tugged at her earring ab-sently. Tomiko wore diamond studs, and a woman might rub, push, or scratch them, but a tug? That was a sign.

She gave him her phone number. He didn't offer his. Tomiko went over to her friends, who bubbled with excitement about the handsome man she was with. Luther watched her go but made sure he turned away when she got to her table.

"Nice ass on her," said Frank as he walked up. "No need to let it go for me."

"I didn't," Luther said.

"What did you tell her your name was?"

"Jordan," said Luther.

"Nice. Let's get a table."

Luther and Frank walked over to a raised area up and away from the dance floor and grabbed a little table. There were not many people in this area, as most of the action was focused on the dance floor, the surrounding tables, and the bar. They ordered drinks, and Luther could already tell that Frank was up to some-thing. He was jovial and laughing just a little too much. Frank was very intelligent, but he lacked the one quality that would make him a great agent. He had no instinct, that innate ability to know behavior and how to behave, to see and to hide. He stank at it, so before Sharon Bane walked in, Luther knew he had been set up.

Sharon Bane was pretty and doe-eyed, with a frame that was deceptively feminine. Underneath her all-American, girl-next-door looks was a hard woman who was trained in the deadly arts and bragged that she could bench-press two and a half times her weight.

Sharon was wearing a pair of tight jeans and stiletto-heeled boots. Her top was thin and airy and showed just a hint of her bra underneath. She wore little or no makeup, but her skin was so smooth that it was hard to tell sometimes. Her hair was neatly tied back into her trademark ponytail.

She was a woman of many contrasts. She came from a family of shit-kickers in Missouri, and you could tell that she'd worked hard to cover up her southern accent.

Frank had been trying to get into her pants with no success. Sharon and Luther were friends, and Luther knew that part of Frank's inviting him out tonight was just to make Sharon feel comfortable while he tried to get some drinks into her and then get himself into her.

"Hey, Luther," said Sharon. She hugged him tightly, patting him on the back.

She hugged Frank as well, but there was a world of difference in her manner. She seemed to like him but was made uncomfortable by his attraction to her, or perhaps it was the fact that he couldn't hide his attraction. Luther found her alluring, as any man would, but he had instinct, and he turned his attraction off whenever she was around. It seemed foul to like Sharon. It was like dating your sister.

They made small talk for a while, Sharon telling them about a drug cartel in Argentina that had met an untimely demise. Luther talked about a fire in Stockholm.

Frank brought up the Homeland Security Act. The act was a joke, a political trick intended mostly to allow government agencies more power and money to do their jobs. E-1 had gotten a load of cash from the HSA, and so the agency would soon be upgraded in all areas.

"So, Luther," Sharon began, "I'm sure you know this was not really a social call tonight."

Luther nodded, and Frank seemed to be taken off guard. Luther didn't look at him as his face fell into a subtly quizzical look to cover the obvious truth Sharon was telling. It was good and would have fooled a layman, but to Luther it was just more evidence that Frank didn't speak the language that he and Sharon Bane did.

"Well, we really wanted to hang with you, Luth," Frank stumbled.

A very pregnant moment passed; then Sharon sighed a little. "He's way ahead of us, Frank," said Sharon. "He knows why we asked him here. Don't you, Luther?" She smiled at her friend.

Luther had surmised this a long time ago but was hoping that they would lose their nerve. He should have known better of Sharon. She had once shot herself in the side to avoid blowing her cover. She was fearless.

"You two want to know what the director said to me," said Luther. "And since we all generally respect an agent's right to privacy, I assume you have some interest in whatever assignment, if any, the director gave me. If that were the case, sadly, I would have to decline."

Sharon just stared at Luther with intensity. It was as if they were reading each other's minds. Luther stared back, and in that moment something did pass between them, an understanding born of their shared instinct.

"I'm sorry, Luther," said Sharon. "But we know that the staff has been processing a lot of nationwide intel on local law enforcement, which leads us to believe that there's something big going on."

"And if it's big," said Frank, "you might need help."

"It's cool," said Luther. He wasn't angry with them. "I understand. "Well, if that's all . . ."

"Wait," said Frank. "The discussion can't be over."

"Thanks for asking me out, guys," said Luther. "I'll be in touch."

"Okay, Luther," said Sharon, and the guilt over trying to compromise her friend's mission was in her voice. Luther hugged her in a forgiving manner, and when he let her go, she looked better.

Frank was ready to protest. Obviously he'd brought this whole thing about. He had come to the X Club to get information on Luther's assignment and get Sharon Bane into bed. In his mind one was linked to the other. He'd crack Luther, Sharon would be grateful, and before she knew it, he'd be between her legs. Now he saw both prizes slipping away. He didn't protest, however. He just remained silent.

Luther finished his drink and then descended the riser back to the bar and dance floor. He searched for Tomiko, but she was gone. He gave the place the once-over, then left. Tomiko's party was still chattering at a table, so he figured she had decided to find some other man interesting and go home with him.

He was a little surprised when he went out to the valet and found her waiting for him.

"Your friends are long-winded," she said.

"I was headed home," said Luther. He gave the valet his ticket.

"Are you sure that beautiful girl you were with in there won't mind?" she asked.

"You don't seem like the jealous type," he said.

"And you never answer a question directly." Tomiko moved closer to him, nestling under his arm. "Maybe you'll be more talkative tomorrow morning."

They didn't talk much on the way back to Luther's place. Tomiko rubbed his leg and pulled his hand under her skirt while he drove. It was elegant the way she did it, as if she'd done it before, but not with just anyone.

They got to his condo and went inside the building under the watchful eye of the guard at the door. Luther very badly wanted to kiss her, but he didn't really like public displays of affection. Tomiko controlled herself as well, and it only made what was coming more exciting for them both.

When Luther got to his door, Tomiko pulled him to her and kissed him hard. He gave in for a moment and then moved to find his keys. She pulled his hand to her breast, as if sensing that he was going to do some other silly thing with it.

Luther was letting go, wanting her body and the lovely, sweet abandon it would bring. Then all his instincts were immediately turned back on.

The polycord on the doorjamb was broken.

Luther pushed Tomiko away a little too hard. He moved back and assumed a slightly crouched posture. How stupid he'd been, he thought. He knew that desire was the most potent of all disablers, and no matter how many times you read the E-1 manual, no matter how many courses in counteragent methods you took, you lost IQ points when your dick got stiff.

"What's wrong?" asked Tomiko breathlessly.

Luther didn't answer. He just watched her standing there looking gorgeous and confused. Did she know that his place had been compromised? Did she kiss him because she wanted to fuck him or because she wanted him to go inside without seeing that the polycord seal had been broken? Luther's face fell into a flat, dangerous look, the look that said he was about to do violence, and Tomiko unconsciously took a step backward.

If she was going to do something, it would happen right now, Luther thought, and he'd have to respond quickly and cleanly. He had a backup weapon, an S&W shorty .40 in an ankle holster. The P99 was too big to hide under his clothes. He'd have to drop her before she could reach hers. But Tomiko just kept looking at him with innocence and fear in her eyes. The moment was heavy, but he did not sense danger from her.

Luther quickly assessed the situation and began to relax. If Tomiko was out to get him, she could have done so many times in the car or at the club. She was just what he thought she was: a beautiful woman who wanted to sleep with him.

"I'm okay," said Luther. "But I don't think it's a good idea for you to stay tonight."

"Are you married or something?" she asked with a tiny bit of disappointment in her voice.

"No, I'm not," he responded calmly. "Look, the guard downstairs will call a car for you. I'm sorry, Tomiko, really."

Tomiko was struck silent. Luther could see so many things going through her head: Was he lying? Was he gay? Was he crazy?

She stood straight and then walked over to him, placing a small kiss on his cheek.

"Take care, Jordan," she said. And she said his name as if she wasn't sure it was his real name. She had intuition, too, this woman, and he was deeply sorry to see her move away from him. He wanted to grab her, to forget who and what he was, but that feeling was buried under a mountain of training and discipline.

Luther watched her walk off. When he was sure she was gone, he pulled the shorty .40 and went inside. He moved into the little hallway off the front door. He knew that if there were someone still inside, he would have to show himself soon or the element of surprise would be lost. Who would be foolish enough to try to take down an E-1 agent in D.C.? Not many, Luther thought, but that didn't stop him from moving into the living room, then into the bedrooms and kitchen, looking for intruders. He checked each closet and even the ledge outside the window. He made a thorough sweep and even did a quick electronic scan for devices. It was all clear.

But someone had been inside his place, he thought. Luther turned off all the lights, went into his utility area, and removed a pair of thermal readout glasses. Through the glasses Luther could now see impressions of depth and temperature. The glasses were effective, but they hurt his eyes like all hell.

Luther saw his own depression tracks. Temperature readings showed pink where he had pressed his hands just moments before. Then he saw them—foot impressions left by someone else. The impressions looked to be those of a smaller person. He followed the footprints into his bedroom and saw them stop by his bed.

He saw hand impressions and temperature readings on his

bedcovers. The handprints were thick and rounded at the finger-tips, telling Luther that the intruder had worn gloves. The impressions ended at his pillow.

Luther gently pressed the pillow and heard the soft crinkle of paper as he did. He took off the glasses and lifted the pillow carefully. His eyes adjusted, and the pain stopped as he did.

Under the pillow, written on a piece of plain white paper and printed with care and precision, was this message:

DON'T TAKE THE MISSION.

The Evidence of Nothing

The note that had been secreted into his room was on Luther's mind as he read through the case file on Alex Deavers. He didn't know who had left the missive, and he wasn't going to try to find out right now. That would just slow him down, and if he reported it to Kilmer, it might endanger his status on the mission.

He did surmise that the note writer was an insider, someone who had training and knew how to break into a place virtually undetected. It could have been anybody from E-1, even Kilmer. Hampton was back in the United States, but he was getting ready to accompany Luther on the mission. He ruled Hampton out. Frank and Sharon Bane had both come to the X Club late and were not together, so it could have been either of them.

These were troubling thoughts for Luther, but if the note writer had wanted to do him harm, he or she would have tried.

Luther had gotten up early to read over the file on Deavers's disappearance. They had him tracked fairly well until Canada, and then they'd found the wrong man on a ship. The Canadians had good government agents, and if they'd lost Alex, it was only because he was good, not because they were deficient. The Royal Canadian Mounted Police, Border Police, and the Security Intelligence Review Committee all had good people and expert trackers and fully cooperated with the United States.

If he was going to find Alex Deavers, he'd have to be resourceful. An agent leaves the evidence of nothing, he said again to himself. But that truth was relative. If nothing was left, then no one could ever find an agent. What Deavers had meant was that an agent leaves a trail of *normality*, a statement that things are maybe too right and good.

Luther looked at the ship's log information again. The *Sjø-mannskirken*, a Norwegian freighter, had left Great Britain and had an uneventful journey to a northern Canadian port in the province of Quebec, in Tête-à-la-Baleine. Once it got there, Gustav Brehimson, a man with questionable papers, had gotten off and disappeared. This was the man E-1 thought to be Alex Deavers.

When the man calling himself Brehimson was located, it was discovered that his real name was Norske Svalbard and that he was an illegal immigrant from Norway. Alex was nowhere to be found.

Luther checked again and again, looking for anything he might find. Then, in the captain's supplemental log, a massive pile of paper that contained everything useless that had occurred on the voyage, there was an entry that stood out. Luther didn't know why the entry was not listed separately as a report or put into the main log. He guessed that the captain didn't want to bother with all the paperwork involved. On its second night, the *Sjømannskirken* had been aided by a ship named the *Métier*, a

French vessel headed for the United States. The *Métier* had come upon the *Sjømannskirken* when she had developed engine trouble and had stopped for repairs at sea. The captain of the *Sjømannskirken* had logged information earlier about questionable engines in port. He allowed the other ship to assist, and then both ships had gone on their separate ways. The entry was a single paragraph.

Luther smiled and almost laughed at the simplicity of the event.

That was how Alex had done it.

Alex was indeed on the *Sjømannskirken* as Gustav Brehimson, but he had switched ships. Alex had sabotaged the engine and jumped aboard the Baltimore-bound *Métier*. He'd switched his papers with Norske Svalbard and then vanished. It was a classic E-1 diversion. Alex had gotten information on the *Métier*'s course and planned to have the ships rendezvous. The son of a bitch had gone straight into the States.

Luther's heart began to race. He quickly got on his computer and accessed E-1's mainframe. There he got the information on the *Métier*. It had landed in Baltimore, and only its captain had kept an official record of the midocean encounter.

Alex had sneaked into the country and landed just miles from E-1 itself. It was quintessential agent logic: hide in plain sight.

Luther called Hampton, who praised him on his sleuthing. Then he reported his findings to Kilmer and started planning his trip. He didn't see it done, but he knew as soon as he hung up the phone that his little gold button was moved from Washington, D.C., to Baltimore.

As Luther prepared to go, a thought crept back into his head. It was vague at first and then became focused and intense. The mark of a good agent is that his analytical mind processed information subconsciously. Since Kilmer had said these words, Luther had been haunted by them. It was a slip of the tongue from a man who never slipped, a lapse from a man who could not afford to have gaps in his logic. And for an agent it was undeniably a clue to something.

"*. . . in possession of that information, too.*"

Luther was tracking a dangerous man who held something that the leader of the agency did not want to tell him about. He'd be leaving for Baltimore with more than one mystery on his mind.

Luther

Luther set out that day to make the short drive from D.C. to Baltimore, with Hampton riding shotgun. He and Hampton had done many missions together. They got along fine, but Hampton was a stickler for protocol, and Luther liked to wing it. Once, on an assignment in Korea, Hampton's by-the-book attitude caused them to be discovered, and an ambush was set for them. Luther saw the sign of the trap, but instead of avoiding it, which was the standard policy, he engaged the men and killed them all. Hampton had almost been shot. Afterward they argued bitterly about who was at fault. In Luther's mind Hampton was a stiff, and in Hampton's mind Luther could be a loose cannon. It was a good match.

The black Ford pulsed with the sounds of Biggie Smalls. The rearview mirror vibrated with the thick bass.

"Do we have to listen to that stuff all the time?" asked Hampton, referring to the music. "I know it gets you in the mood, but it just gives me a headache."

"Sorry, but I need my music."

"Would a little Coldplay kill you?"

"Yes, it would," said Luther. He actually liked the group, but he was a creature of habit. "You always complain about the music. I would think that by now you would've established an appreciation."

"It's all derivative imitation, and you know it. Hip-hop is the beginning of the end of society."

They laughed, and Luther drove on. To anyone on the freeway, they could have been two friends off to a fun weekend, not two men looking for a third man who had to be killed.

"Do you think anyone else knows about our mission?" asked Luther.

"No, but it's not impossible that someone would know," said Hampton. "Even secret agencies have leaks. Why? Someone say something to you?"

"No," said Luther. He started to tell Hampton about the note but thought better of it.

Hampton flipped open a laptop computer and accessed the mainframe. Luther saw a map of Baltimore pop on-screen. Then the screen split, and a list of weapons and devices appeared. Hampton was mapping out a strategy and scenarios for finding Alex. That's why he was the best TWA in E-1. He was always thinking ahead.

Luther let Hampton go to his business and immersed himself in the throbbing bass of the song. He was in full mission mode now, ready for anything.

Luther Martin Green had been born into a normal midwestern family. His parents, Roland and Theresa, were both from the South—Kentucky and New Orleans, respectively. Roland and

Theresa had five children: Micah James, Ruth Ann, Thomas Paul, Mary Theresa, whom they all called Mary Sunshine because of her fascination with shiny objects, and finally Luther.

Like most people in Detroit, the home they made in the North was just a transplanted southern one. They struggled financially but always managed to keep the family afloat.

Luther was a tiny thing when he was born, and his mother had nicknamed him Cricket because of this. But as he grew up, it soon became obvious that young Luther was an exceptional human being. He seemed to know things before they were taught, and that which was instructed was learned immediately. He was talking and reading early and before long had plowed his way through every book in the house.

Theresa and Roland were of course proud of their son. So within the limits of their financially challenged lives, they steered resources toward the bright young man.

Luther breezed through a special prep school for gifted students and later Cass Tech High in Detroit.

In high school he met Vanessa Brown, a sweet little junior who was every bit as smart as he was. She was a book nerd but cute as she could be, and she always had a smile on her face. They bonded, sharing dreams and sweet kisses, and one night when her parents were away, they made love for the first time with each other.

After high school Luther attended West Point, scoring top marks in academics, military training, and sports. And for the first time in his life, he met people who were smarter and more accomplished in certain fields.

But while he was outmatched in some areas, no one in the institution had all the qualities he did. No one except Sharon

Bane. Sharon was the female Luther. Born to a trailer-trash family, she was a rebel and had all the talent to back it up. They became fast friends, their difference in race and gender quelling any rivalry they might have had.

Luther graduated with honors and planned to go into the Army Rangers to serve out his commission. These plans were changed when a government man came to visit. The man came each year, and each year it was rumored that he selected recruits for special assignment. Luther had never paid much attention to the rumors, but that year, after the visit, he was called in to a meeting and was surprised to see Sharon Bane and another cadet, Henry Trenchant, both of whom had also graduated at the top of their class. They were told that they would receive a special commission to work with an unclassified agency. The school did not know anything about the government man or whom he represented. It was widely rumored that the CIA or NSA was behind this.

Luther and Sharon took the offer. Henry did not and was sworn never to breathe a word of it afterward.

Luther, Sharon, and several others from Annapolis, the U.S. Air Force Academy, and the Marine Corps Recruit Depot at Parris Island were trained in secret for three years. They learned various forms of martial arts and were schooled in weapons use and explosives. The training was grueling and relentless. Eventually Luther and the others were removed from their units altogether and trained full-time.

Luther soon understood that this special unit was not the CIA. The men who trained them seemed concerned primarily with methods of elimination. Even before they told him, he knew he was being trained as an assassin.

This was when Luther met Alex Deavers. Alex's arrival was heralded as the make-or-break point of the cadets' training.

He arrived during their fight instruction one cold day in Virginia. The cadets were randomly sparring when Deavers, clad in a crisp navy suit, entered the facility and assumed a fighting pose. The other instructors backed away, leaving the cadets to face the lone man five to one.

Deavers approached the fist cadet, a young man named Tony Andrisi. Tony was generally agreed to be the best fighter of the group. Deavers faked a punch. Andrisi lifted his hands in defense and then delivered a kick that Deavers easily dodged. Then Deavers threw a punch at Andrisi that was so fast Luther thought it was another bluff, but the blow hit Andrisi on the temple and dropped him to one knee.

Andrisi was about to move when Deavers said, "Get up and I'll kill you." Andrisi stayed down.

Deavers put down Sharon and the other two cadets in similar fashion, each time faking an assault, then countering the aggression with a punch or kick that was too fast to defend.

Deavers got to Luther, and Luther swore he could see the shadow of a smile on his lips. Luther stood fast and then searched Deavers's face. Their eyes locked, and Luther saw something that set him at ease. Deavers raised a leg and aimed a side kick at Luther's head. Luther barely dodged the assault but did not attack. Deavers then executed a series of moves, and Luther struggled to survive them. Finally Luther landed a punch, but Deavers swept his legs from under him, ending the contest.

"Fighting is not about hurting your enemy; it's about understanding him, then killing him," Deavers had said. "This cadet avoided my assault as best he could until he saw a weakness. But of course he had the advantage of seeing the rest of you fail, didn't he?" And now Deavers did smile.

That day the cadets were told something of the institution called E-1. They were given as much info as they needed, which was not much. Luther surmised that he was being trained to kill, and the prospect excited and terrified him.

During the next year, Luther was taken under Deavers's wing and forged into another person. Deavers liked Luther's youth and brashness. The young kid soaked up everything Deavers had to offer, learning the history of the agency and its secrets and memorizing the E-1 rule book, the blueprint for their future.

Luther also learned to focus his anger and aggression into useful energy. Deavers trained him and the others to look at their exceptional status as human beings in a new way. They were elite and had to remain unburdened by the false morality of common people. They were being trained to eliminate the enemies of their country. They were machines to this end, and duty, honor, and patriotism were their fuel.

Luther was accepted into E-1 at the age of twenty-one, the youngest agent in the agency's history. He was given a document called the *vita pactum*, a simple one-page document in which the agent promised to give his life to the agency, and in return the agency would always take care of his every need. Luther signed it and was married to E-1 forever.

Luther took to his new job with the same fierceness and brilliance with which he did everything else. Alex Deavers saw to it that Luther was not wasted in his new occupation. He sent Luther on a mission the first week after his graduation.

Luther was dispatched to Germany to neutralize an arms dealer who'd become troublesome to peace negotiations in

Eastern Europe. Luther knew nothing of him until he got there. When he received the file, he saw that the man, Caesar Reniddo, was a former army lieutenant trained in fighting and weapons. He was also a black man.

That was Alex, Luther had thought. He wanted to test Luther in every way, including his racial loyalty.

Luther neutralized Reniddo and his two bodyguards on his first night in the country. The bodyguards were killed with a silenced weapon. Reniddo's throat was cut as he slept. Luther felt a great rush of emotion at his first kills. He was excited, guilty, sickened, and empowered by the feeling. It was like hearing bright music crescendo, then recede into silence—the cold, deep space of the human heart.

Luther left an angry note, handwritten in Lebanese. The authorities made the normal assumptions, and the matter was closed. After that first assignment, Luther had gone on mission after mission, building his skill and confidence. His former life became a distant, faded dream, hidden under layers of missions and aliases and secrets. Detroit, his family, and the young, sweet Vanessa and the Cricket were ghosts locked in some faraway country. There were women, but they never lasted long; and there were friends, but they were all within the structure of E-1's family. The agency became his life.

Luther became one of Alex Deavers's killing machines, a man possessed of deadly skill and cold, controlled emotion. He often wondered which was deadlier, the blow that killed or the lack of emotion that catalyzed it.

Luther also became a patriot. Most Americans didn't know the price of freedom, but he did. He'd visited the ghettos and hellholes of the world and had seen the look of loss and need in the eyes of the hungry and dying that would make a common homeless man's stare look like a smile. Americans went through their privileged lives not knowing why they had cars, skyscrapers, NBA teams, and thirty-one flavors. Someone else in the world paid the price for our advantages, usually with their lives.

Luther believed in America, but he was practical about it. If his country wasn't the leader of the world, another country would have assumed the position, and it would be no less protective of its interests. A true patriot knew that everything in life was the lesser of two evils.

This was how he and the other E-1 agents justified their occupation. The men and women they eliminated were plagues on humanity. If they were allowed to live, they would undoubtedly cause the deaths of countless innocents. So by terminating them, they actually saved lives.

"Exit," he heard Hampton say.

"Got it," he said almost at the same time.

They were in sync as usual, he thought. He felt the music merge with his excitement as the Ford Explorer rolled off an exit and into the city of Baltimore, where he hoped that his mission would end quickly with the elimination of Alex Deavers.

East Baltimore

Luther and Hampton sat in the Ford and watched ships unload at East Baltimore's Inner Harbor. The sun was out, but it was blocked by hazy clouds that made everything seem dismal and gray. Besides, it was nearing the horizon. Soon it would set, and the night would rise, taking the town to darkness.

The area was generally unkempt, and the steady wind was filled with the smell of fish and the ocean. Something about this place unsettled Luther. He didn't know whether it was instinct or the fact that he hadn't been in America in a long time, but something had his mind on a yellow alert.

Luther was settled near Wagner's Point in Baltimore. That's where the *Métier* had come into port.

Dockworkers hurried about with a measured energy that suggested they had a long time to work and a short time to live. Luther remembered that feeling, the state of normality enjoyed by ordinary people. It seemed so distant now in his world.

He was trying to figure out what Alex Deavers was thinking when he so cleverly deceived them by switching ships. Of course he was covering his tracks, but with the government's information-gathering ability, it seemed an almost impossible task to get away cleanly. Still, Alex was too smart to have randomly chosen this city. It was too close to D.C., too close to E-1, to be anything but a calculated effort. Again, the question was why.

"I know that the wolf came here because it was the last place we'd expect him to," said Hampton. "But that couldn't have been the only reason."

"If I know Alex, he had something hidden here," said Luther. "Money, a contact, maybe a weapon."

"God, I hope it's not one of *my* weapons," said Hampton.

Luther pictured Alex sneaking off the boat, paying off whoever had assisted him, then getting transportation. And Deavers had covered his tracks well. The locals and the FBI hadn't found a single person willing to admit that he'd seen anyone fitting Alex's unique description. And who wouldn't remember a disfigured man?

Hampton turned on his laptop, which was nestled securely in a holder built in to the dashboard. He pulled up the E-1 Operations Mission Program, called EOPM.

"What's it say?" asked Luther, aware of what Hampton was doing.

"Most of the men interviewed were telling the truth about Deavers, all but one. A man named Kraemer was noted as 'suspicious' by the maritime authorities, the FBI, and the Harbor Patrol. Kraemer was part of the *Métier*'s rescue team when it came upon the *Sjømannskirken* at sea."

"But his story checked out," said Luther.

"It did, but two men on the *Métier* noted that Kraemer had disappeared for a time after the ship was under way again."

Hampton pulled up a picture of Kraemer. He was a round little white man whose features were doughy and bland. His skin was ruddy from years at sea, and his head was a mess of dark, greasy hair.

"A handsome figure of a man," said Hampton.

"He's our target. He'll lead us to something."

"You mean to the wolf."

"I don't think Alex is here anymore," said Luther. "It's been too long, and I know *I* wouldn't sit so close to D.C. for an extended period of time."

They soon spotted Kraemer, who looked just like his picture. When he left work, Luther followed him away from the pier and into the city. Luther hit the Ford's CD player, and Outkast blasted from the speakers. The thick bass and Andre 3000's rapid-fire rap filled him with energy.

"You're going to kill me before the wolf," said Hampton.

Kraemer made a pit stop at a 7-Eleven and came out with a plastic bag holding a six-pack of beer. Kraemer got into his car, popped the top on a can, and drank.

"Not a very safe driver," said Luther.

Kraemer pulled away. Luther waited a moment and then followed. Although Luther didn't know the region, he did know that East Baltimore was the black part of the city and considered to be a dangerous area. That's where Kraemer headed.

Luther's mind worked as he trailed Kraemer into the heart of the inner city, watching the faces turn from white to black and the sky fill with darkness.

The streets in a place like this came to life at night. This didn't unsettle Luther; it stimulated him. There would be danger, and he was ready. So far this whole wolf chase had been a mental cat-and-mouse game. He was definitely due for some real action.

A startling thought occurred to Luther. Could Alex still be in the city? Was this a trap of some kind? Luther got excited for just a moment; then he calmed down.

"He's going into the inner city," said Hampton. "What's a white guy gonna do there?"

"I don't know. Any man can get into a lot of trouble in the 'hood," said Luther.

Kraemer stopped his vehicle in front of a run-down, blasted-out building near East Fayette and North Port streets. Although Luther had never been here, he sensed that it was not a safe place.

Luther and Hampton watched as Kraemer got out, slipped what had to be money to two young black men, and went inside. The money, Luther knew, was payment for them to watch Kraemer's car, a brand-new Volvo, much too nice a car to be in this part of town at night.

Luther rolled by the building, and the two black men gave his vehicle more than a passing look. He drove for another two blocks, then turned around and headed back. The streets had the look of an urban war zone and reminded him a great deal of Detroit.

"So what's Kraemer doing here?" asked Hampton.

"More important, what does his presence have to do with Alex Deavers, if anything?"

Luther parked his Ford in the well-lit lot of a restaurant not too far from where Kraemer was. Hampton removed his sidearm, a 9mm Baby Eagle, and made sure it was loaded.

Luther took a few steps away, then spoke. "You got me?" he asked.

"Yep," said Hampton, and Luther heard him clearly in a small earpiece he wore.

Luther took his P99 and proceeded back to the building where Kraemer had gone on foot. He was wearing jeans and a black hooded sweatshirt. He'd fit right in.

Luther walked the three blocks back to the building. With each step he grew more energized and more dangerous. The ghetto was just another kind of mission terrain, he reasoned. London, Prague, or East Baltimore—the mission was the same, and the rules and objectives still applied.

"If Deavers isn't here, as you suggest," said Hampton, "we only need minimal effort."

"And what the hell does that mean?" asked Luther.

"Try not to kill anyone," said Hampton.

"Not making any promises."

As Luther approached the building, he hoped the Volvo would still be there. It was. The two men were still watching the car, but now they were on the stoop of the building.

Luther saw that they were hard street types, the kind of men who'd probably do anything for money. He debated buying them off but didn't trust them to take his bribe. In most cases guys like this would just decide to rob him and stay loyal to their employer, in which case he'd have to kill them. He didn't want that. Still, he would have to engage them in order to find out why Kraemer was in this neighborhood and in this building.

"Two men in my way," said Luther.

The street was desolate. It still smelled like some kind of trap, but Luther pressed on. He moved closer, and the two men saw him. If one of them bolted for the building, he'd have to move fast. But they didn't. To them Luther was just another brother from the 'hood, someone they had no fear of. They had beaten and probably killed men who looked more dangerous than Luther. The men had no way of knowing that the man walking toward them could bring quick and sudden death.

One of them stood. He was of medium build and appeared to be only twenty or so. The other man was bigger and looked much more dangerous. That's the one Luther wanted. In multiple-adversary combat, it was axiomatic that the larger of the two was usually the greater threat. If Luther could subdue the big man, the smaller one would feel vulnerable and would be easier to defeat. And it was always best to expend your freshest energy on the bigger man.

Luther stopped a few feet from the standing man. He was wearing an Orioles baseball cap and a dirty gray T-shirt. The bigger man was wearing a blue Phat Farm sweatshirt. He just sat and watched, scowling.

"Keep walkin', nigga," said the man in the gray shirt. His voice was thin but measured and very confident. "Nuthin' for ya 'round here, playa."

Luther remained silent. And he did keep walking, right over to the other man. The big man stood up, but before he could react, Luther moved in and delivered a slashing blow to his throat. The man grabbed his neck, and Luther swept his legs from under him. The big man fell and hit the stoop hard, his head slamming on the bottom step. He was still clutching his neck and bleeding a little from the side of his head.

Luther had turned while sweeping the big man, and when he was done, he faced Mr. Gray Shirt. The smaller man was reaching into his pants. Luther pulled his P99 and held it right in front of the man's face. Gray Shirt stopped, and Luther easily disarmed him of the gun he'd been going for.

Luther pushed Gray Shirt toward the fallen man and then pulled the fallen man's gun from his waistband. He put both guns into the pouch of his sweatshirt.

"You a cop?" asked Gray Shirt.

"The white man," said Luther, ignoring him. "Who is he, and why is he here?"

"Fuck you," said Gray Shirt.

Luther stepped around Gray Shirt and kicked the big man in the jaw, breaking it. The sound made Gray Shirt flinch. Luther repeated his question.

"I don't know!" said Gray Shirt. "He just started coming here and paid us to watch his car. He stay here all night, and then he leave."

"What room is he in?" asked Luther.

"He up on the second floor, first door. Don't nobody live in the place, man. It used to be a rock house, but—"

Luther didn't need to hear the rest of the statement. He punched Gray Shirt in the ribs, knocking the air out of him. Then he slammed his forearm into his jaw, and the man dropped to the ground. Luther took the bullets from their guns and tossed them, and then he tossed the guns into the sewer grate at the curb.

"And no one's dead," Luther said to Hampton. "See how nice I can be?"

"Excellent," said Hampton. "I can't wait to find out Kraemer's situation."

Luther entered the building. The odor of decay and urine assaulted him. Dried blood and gang signs covered the wall of the stairwell he ascended. His mind was filling with memories of his life on the streets of Detroit. He'd been in many places like this. He'd watched them turn from homes filled with love and hope to abandoned shells, haunted by the ghosts of destroyed lives.

Luther got to the landing and approached the first door. He had to act quickly. This was looking more and more like some kind of setup.

Luther kicked in the flimsy door and entered with his P99 in hand. Kraemer turned and was startled, dropping his beer to the floor. He got up from the chair he'd been sitting in.

"About time," said Kraemer.

"Don't speak unless I ask you a question," said Luther.

Kraemer said nothing. Luther looked around for a second, then back to Kraemer.

"I'm only going to ask you once," said Luther. "Who sent you here?"

"A man named Luther Green," said Kraemer.

Luther almost lowered his gun. Alex. He knew. Somehow he knew that Luther would be sent after him.

"And why did he send you here?"

"He said you'd know. Said you two worked together for Immigration and were on the trail of some bad men. I didn't believe him at first. I mean, he looked like hell; his face was all mangled. He said he got that in Desert Storm. I was in the service, too, the marines."

"What else did he say to you?" asked Luther, and now he almost wanted to laugh at the use of his name. Alex had not completely lost his mind. He still had a sense of irony.

"He gave me a lot of money and told me to keep coming here until a black man showed up asking questions," said Kraemer. "You're here, so I'm out."

Luther read the man. He was scared of what he was doing, yet he seemed a little relieved to see Luther.

"Why here?" Luther asked, almost to himself.

"Said you'd know that, too. Look, I did what he asked. Can I go now? I hate this place, and them guys outside are gonna jack me sooner or later, I just know it."

"How long was he here?" asked Luther.

"A few days. Luther found this place. Look, I thought he was some kind of stowaway, but he had government ID, and he said he was working on something big. I don't want no trouble, you know? I was trying to help my country."

"Think carefully," said Luther. "Did he say anything else, anything at all?"

"No, but he did make me take him down to Veterans' Hall one day. He went in empty-handed and came out the same way, but he seemed to be different when he came out."

"Different how?"

"I dunno. Happy, pleased about something. And I didn't ask him nothing. The man didn't like questions, and I ain't stupid."

Luther lowered his weapon and told Kraemer to go, thanking him on behalf of Immigration. He also told him to wake up the two men outside, tell them that the cops would be here shortly, and to leave if they knew what was good for them.

Kraemer ran out, and Luther inspected the room. When he heard Kraemer's car pull off, he went down and checked the street. They were all gone.

"Now what?" asked Hampton, who had heard everything.

"I check the room," said Luther. "Then we go to Veterans' Hall tomorrow."

Luther went back to the room and found a few answers to his many questions.

"Why did he use your name?" asked Hampton.

"To prove that he knew E-1 was on the case and had figured

out his deception. Why he felt so sure I would be sent, I don't know."

"Well, I know why the wolf chose East Baltimore. The government's informational power is great, but only in large metropolitan areas or in places of affluence. It's weakened in the areas of American life we care the least about."

"The ghetto is a no-man's-land to the government. Alex taught me that at E-1."

Luther looked all over the small space again. There was only the bed and a little nightstand, so there was really nowhere to hide anything.

Luther swept the room three times but found nothing. He was about to leave when he stopped and laughed at himself, looking up at the ceiling. An old ball-shaped light fixture threw a sick yellowish illumination into the room. He saw something in the bulb. It was dark, and it looked like a sliver of fallen plaster.

"Got something," said Luther.

He stepped up on the chair and unscrewed the light fixture. Inside, he found a four-megabyte Sony memory stick, the kind used in digital recorders.

"It's a memory stick," said Luther.

"A message?" asked Hampton.

"Presumably."

From outside, Luther heard a car roar up, burning rubber. Taking a quick glance out the window, he saw the men he'd put down get out of a GMC truck with three other men.

"My friends are back," he said.

"Get the hell out of there," said Hampton.

Luther pocketed the memory stick and then moved out. There were too many of them for him to avoid casualties, he thought. He heard them coming up the front stairs and headed toward the back. As he made it to the rear, he could hear them going into the room he'd just come out of.

Luther pulled his gun and moved toward the rear door. He would run back to his truck and be gone before they knew anything.

But as he moved into the backyard, Luther felt a hand grab his gun hand. He turned just in time to catch the thick end of a baseball bat in his other hand. It was the big man Luther had put down earlier. They struggled with each other as Luther saw behind the big man a new one, a dark man with dreadlocks—holding a long machete.

"Move!" said the man with the machete. He voice was rich with a Caribbean accent, and he was trying to chop Luther with the large blade.

Luther kept the big man between him and the machete as they struggled. The big man shifted his weight onto Luther and forced Luther to let go of his gun to keep his balance. Luther dropped it into some thick weeds. He lifted his knee into the big man's groin, and the man let go of the bat. Luther gave the big man an elbow to the side of the head, sending him stumbling to one side.

The dreadlocked man quickly advanced with the blade, but suddenly two loud pops sounded behind Luther, and the man was hit in the chest. Luther turned to see Hampton, with a gun, out in front.

Luther went back to the big man and finished him with a series of punches to the face, then found his gun and ran to the far end of the yard where Hampton was waiting.

"Thought you needed help," said Hampton.

"I had it under control," said Luther.

Right then a shot rang out, just missing them. They looked up and saw a man holding a gun leaning from a window on the second floor. Luther and Hampton swiftly moved away and ran off before they got another bead drawn on them.

They moved as fast as they could back to the Ford, got in, and drove away.

Silence permeated the car for a while. Luther was clearly upset. Hampton looked a little shaken but seemed basically calm.

"You okay?" he asked.

"Yes," said Luther. "Why did you do that?"

"I could hear the struggle. It didn't sound like it was going good. I made a judgment."

"If I needed help, I would've asked for it," said Luther. He was upset, but Hampton might just have saved his life. "Nice shot," Luther conceded, smiling. "That a new gun?"

"Baby Eagle, nine-millimeter," said Hampton. "I wanted something with more punch. I modified it with a little computerized balancer that steadies it. I was third in my marksmanship class, you know."

"The guy who just got shot sure knows."

"You think he's dead?" asked Hampton. There was a note of concern in his voice.

"Maybe," said Luther. "You hit him high, though, and he was a big fella, so it could go either way."

Hampton only nodded. He seemed just a little rattled by what could have been his first kill. "So let's hear that recording," he said to change the subject.

Luther drove to a side street some miles away, and Hampton opened his laptop and placed the memory stick inside. Alex

Deavers's voice sounded on the tiny speakers. It was familiar to Luther but had a rough, scratchy edge to it now.

"*I assume that your orders are to eliminate me,*" he began. "*I'd expect as much from Kilmer. In a way it's a sign of respect. I've already died once, so it won't really matter.*" There was a brief silence and then: "*I could tell you why I'm doing this, but I'm sure this recording will find its way to E-1, and I don't want them to know how much I know. The agency tried to eliminate me, and now that they've failed, it's fallen to you. I'd ask you to turn back, but I know you won't. It's too late anyway. Your life is now probably worth about as much as mine.*" More silence. Then: "*If I were you, I'd kill my TWA,*" he said casually. "*More than likely he cannot be trusted.*"

Luther resisted the urge to look at Hampton. He felt Hampton stiffen beside him.

"*My mission is paramount to all others,*" said Alex on the recording. "*So if you persist, I will kill you.*"

The recording ended. Luther played it again, this time trying to see whether there were any nuances he'd missed. There were none. Alex sounded cold and determined, just the way Luther felt on the inside.

"He's insane," said Hampton.

"Because he wants you dead?" asked Luther. He smiled at Hampton.

"Not remotely funny," said Hampton. "He wants to kill us both. And it's standard procedure to try to turn members of a team against each other."

"He referred to E-1 as 'them,' " said Luther. "Does that mean he's allied with our enemies?"

"Possibly," said Hampton. "We have to get that recording to

E-1 for analysis. I'm sure I heard background noises that can be pulled up. Maybe we can figure out where he made it."

"I wouldn't get my hopes too high," said Luther.

Hampton dialed in to E-1 to transmit a digital copy of the recording.

Luther watched his partner and tried to get his head back into the mission, but the confidence with which his prey had called for the death of Hampton echoed persistently in his mind.

Encounter

Alex Deavers's body flew out of the transport. For a moment he felt powerful, as if he'd lift into the air and keep flying forever. Then something slammed into his body. Wind exploded from his lungs, and he heard the distant sound of his own voice.

When at last he descended, he fell through thick bush, which slowed his body and finally deposited him on his back.

He was motionless for a moment. And then he felt something. His hand. There was something moving inside it. He glanced over and saw he was still gripping the secretary's briefcase.

In the distance he heard yelling and gunshots. Gorman was disposing of the others who were not yet dead. When they didn't find him, they'd come looking.

Slowly Alex moved. Then he stood and was hit with a wave of pain that sent him back down. He dropped the briefcase. The left side of his body was burning. His left arm was fractured and his left leg was sprained badly, but he was alive, or at least he thought he was.

He heard the bushes rustle. They were coming, he thought. Gorman and whoever was with him were coming to find and kill him.

Alex grabbed the case and got to his feet. He fought off the dizziness, then walked as fast as he could through the dense cover. He struggled with a sickness he felt rumbling in his belly.

He felt his foot hit the ground, and it gave way a little. He'd stepped on the side of a small hill. He bent down and saw two holes in the side of the hill, partially obscured by some tall grass.

The men were moving closer.

Alex quickly ran to the other side of the hill. He got on his knees and felt around the front of the mound. He found a flap of earth and grass. It looked natural but did not feel that way. He pulled on it, and a door opened up. It was a military field bunker. The soldiers dug them, mapped them, and used them to hide away from enemies.

Alex crawled inside and went to the other end, where the holes were. He waited. Soon men moved by, looking around. He heard Gorman's voice yelling, cursing, trying to find him.

Alex lay still. He fought the pain in his body as the men moved on. He hoped none of the locals with Gorman were military who knew about the bunker. Soon he felt dizzy again, and darkness overtook him. His last thought was that he still had the case.

These images gripped Alex Deavers as he walked along a street in South Philly. He was hurting all over. His body had been aching constantly since he'd been blown from the secretary's plane in Africa. He was taking a variety of medications, but the pain seemed to come and go as it pleased. Then again, his sources for the medicine were not exactly the best. You could get anything on the streets, but you took your chances. He'd never been made sick by any of the bootleg meds, so all in all it was good. He'd rather the stuff not work than be laced with poison.

Alex had opened the secretary's briefcase, and there in the jungle he had learned the awful truth. He knew what he had to do. He'd never been a religious man, but he was certain that having his life spared was some kind of divine act. He had a mission, and this time it did not come from men. He'd been saved from death to avenge a wrong and perhaps redeem his own troubled soul.

Alex had gone to a nearby village and rested and healed with the help of a local family. When he was strong enough, he went after Gorman. He covered himself as best he could, hiding his scarred face with a hooded robe and then later a surgical mask. The mask was great. People kept far away from him, fearing he had something contagious.

It wasn't hard to track his prey. To get out of Africa and elude the government, Gorman had gone through Egypt, where there were many people who would help you for a price. There Alex had found evidence that Gorman was in Germany.

In Germany, Alex found security tight because of terrorist threats. But he was adept at slipping checkpoints, and he kept away from crowded places.

He'd found Gorman in the home of a high-class prostitute. Luckily the woman wasn't home when Alex got there. Alex subdued Gorman and then tried to get information from him. Gorman was tough, but after having all the toes on his right foot smashed with a hammer one by one, his tongue loosened.

Gorman had been paid to kill the secretary by some men who said they worked for a Syrian national. He didn't believe them. He thought they were fronting for someone else, but he didn't care. Gorman was tired of his life in federal service and wanted to retire while he was still young, so he took the loot and helped hatch the plan.

Gorman didn't have any relevant information on the men, and Alex believed him. No good agent would ever give his name or a traceable alias. But the whole thing stank of a government op, and the most damning piece of evidence Gorman gave up was that the men who'd paid him insisted that the briefcase the secretary had carried had to be destroyed, along with its contents.

Alex interrogated Gorman for a while longer, getting the number of the account where his blood money was deposited. Once Alex had verified that the funds were there and made arrangements to access them himself, he killed Gorman as slowly as he could.

Alex then got a local surgeon to work on his face and fix it as best he could. It was a meatball job, and he still looked as if the left side of his face had been caught in some kind of machinery, but it was better than it had been. After the surgery Alex left Germany for Britain. This trip was not an easy one. E-1 had eyes and ears all over the country, so he had to spend quite a bit of Gorman's filthy money to swing the escape.

When he got to England, he sought out his old lover, Lisa Radcliff. He found her, and as soon as she was over the shock of his face, he told her the whole story. Lisa had always been a friend and a great agent. He desperately needed an ally, someone to help him with his grand mission. Lisa would understand, he thought. He was wrong.

She tried to talk him into turning himself in, and then she tried to force him. He should have known better. Lisa had a big heart, but she was low on cynicism and was loyal to the agency. He had to put her down. It wasn't easy. Lisa's skills had not diminished over the years, and she hurt him badly before he snapped her neck.

That seemed a long time ago, Alex mused. How long? Months? Weeks? He couldn't completely remember. His mind wasn't what it used to be, since the accident. No, since the *attempted murder*, he corrected. They tried to backwash me, he thought. He still had trouble believing it.

Alex now walked the nighttime streets of Philadelphia. It was dark, and he preferred to travel at night, for obvious reasons. He wore a black coat and a black fedora with a wide brim. He moved quickly, not stopping to notice or be noticed. The night was cool, and there were never many people about after sundown.

Alex headed south. He didn't like to drive, and it was harder for anyone to keep up with him on foot. If he got stopped by the cops in a car, they might ask questions, and that would lead to fatal consequences. Besides, it was much harder to see the damage to his face in the dark while he was walking and wearing his big hat.

Two young men approached on the other side of the street. They were typical denizens of the inner city: black, loud, and brash. They looked like dealers to Alex, and that was a safe bet.

The two men spotted Alex. One of them whispered something to the other, and they moved across the street, circling behind Alex.

Alex sighed. He didn't need this right now. He was going to get the next piece of information he required and plan the next stage of his mission, and he didn't want to be late.

Behind him Alex heard laughter. They were nearer now, closing on him. If he played their game, this could take all night. He had to dispatch them quickly.

Alex stopped and turned to face the approaching young men. They kept coming, but now they weren't laughing. Their faces looked serious and hard. One of them had a hand inside his jacket.

Alex walked faster, closing the gap. Suddenly he started running toward them. The young men stopped for a moment, frozen by the action.

The one with the gun had it out now, holding it next to his thigh. Alex stopped running at the sight of the weapon. He was too far away, and the young fool might hit him with a lucky shot.

"Whatcha gon' do, nigga?" said the man with the gun. "Give up yo' shit."

Alex stepped closer, letting them get a look at his face.

"Damn," said the man without the gun. "He all fucked up."

Alex took another step forward. He showed no fear and never took his eyes from the men.

"Yo, man, let's go. I think he's crazy," said the man with the gun. Alex saw him put the weapon back into his jacket. "I mean it. Let's bounce."

When the gun was gone, Alex ran to one of the men and slashed at his face. The small knife with the *tanto* tip slashed the man's throat, and a spray of blood shot out. Alex spun, avoiding the blood. The man fell to his knees, trying to stop the flow from his jugular vein.

The other man went for his gun again, but Alex had already moved to him and clamped a hand onto the arm reaching for the weapon. Alex lifted the man's arm, bending it unnaturally. The man yelled as he felt his shoulder strain, and then he screamed as Alex twisted his arm from the socket. Alex finished him by ramming his head into a light pole.

Alex then took the man's gun, pressed it to his chest, and fired once. The sound of the shot was muffled, and the man collapsed to the ground, dead.

Alex wiped the blood from his knife on the fallen man. He checked the one still bleeding. He had slumped face forward and was trying to get to his feet. There was something sick and awful about it. The man struggled to speak as the blood flowed, taking his life with it. He fell onto his nose, and Alex heard it break on the concrete.

He robbed them, taking what little cash and jewelry they had. Then he left the gun nearby and made sure to turn their pockets inside out. The local cops would need help to make this case go away quickly.

Alex ran off, leaving his work behind him. He didn't worry about the carnage. Like most inner cities, South Philly was a great place for an operation. No one cared about the denizens of the inner city, and E-1 had no informational systems here.

He was being smarter with Luther than he was with Lisa. He had tried to reason with Lisa and failed. With Luther he was going about it the right way. An E-1 agent on a killing mission would not believe anything a wolf said to him. But he *would* believe what he felt on a mission. Speaking to Luther through the mission was time-consuming, but Alex hoped it would be worth it. By the time Luther got to him, his former student's keen mind would be tuned to a different frequency from the one E-1 had given him. He'd be ready to know the truth. And if not, then Luther Green would have to die.

South Philly

Luther and Hampton spent the night at an E-1 safe house in Baltimore. Hampton didn't seem rattled by the close call, but he did mention that he was going to phone his girlfriend as soon as he checked stolen-car reports. He and Luther assumed that Alex would follow standard procedure. He'd never rent a car or take any form of public transportation. When on the run, an agent acted like a criminal. Alex had probably stolen a car to make his escape.

Luther settled in with a long session of Beethoven. The music was sweet, but it did not soothe him. As soon as morning broke, Luther checked with Hampton about his work the night before.

"I think I got something," said Hampton.

"Shoot," said Luther.

"Well, there are a lot of stolen-car reports in the last few months, but not many where the cars were recovered in another state."

"Which ones were found in or near an inner city?" asked Luther, trying to hurry this conclusion.

"Five, but only one that wasn't in Baltimore or D.C. It was in Philadelphia."

"That's him," said Luther. "Let's get out of here."

"But don't you think it's . . . ?" Hampton paused and thought a second about what he wanted to say. "The car, it's a solid clue, but it's too solid, too clean. I might even say it's sloppy."

Luther had to agree. Alex could have destroyed the plates and the vehicle's VIN number, switched it or used any number of other methods to throw them off the track. It was like he *wanted* them to follow.

"I see your point," said Luther, "but all we can do is go after him and anticipate that he knows we're coming. Since we know he's baiting us, we now have the upper hand."

"Not necessarily," said Hampton. "If he knows we're coming, then he'll anticipate that *we* know and that we'll try to counter him. He'll have a plan."

"But it won't be as good as ours . . . I hope," said Luther.

Luther and Hampton went to Veterans' Hall in Baltimore first. Hampton confirmed that the building had been a former CIA drop point in the seventies and eighties. After accessing old data files, Luther found what he was looking for. In a basement utility room, he discovered a lockbox built in to a wall. It was plastered over but had been recently uncovered. The box was empty. Alex had taken something from it and gone.

"Why leave Kraemer and the recording?" Luther said.

"For you, it would seem," said Hampton.

"I don't know how to feel about that."

"He's not going down easy," said Hampton. "I think we should consider getting some help on this."

Luther thought about Frank and Sharon and their offer. "No, we can do this," he said.

"I hate it when you use that tone," said Hampton.

"What tone?" asked Luther.

"The black–Clint Eastwood tone."

"If I were the sensitive type, I'd object to the use of my ethnicity as an adjective." Luther smiled a little at his own joke. "And if I'm a black anything, it would be Charles Bronson."

"Bronson?" said Hampton. "Gimme a break."

"He was an assassin, no false sense of nobility, a stone-cold killer. That's me." Luther smiled broadly.

"Sick, sick, man," said Hampton, laughing softly.

Luther and Hampton set off for Philadelphia, which was a quick drive away on I-95. They headed straight for South Philly, where the stolen car had been found. Luther was again reminded of his days on the streets in Detroit. The neighborhood around Seventh Street was run-down, filled with the usual devastation. But it was the faces that really got to Luther, scarred with the plague of hopelessness, haunting.

Luther and Hampton parked on a side street in a very dangerous-looking neighborhood.

"Okay," said Hampton. "This is where the stolen car was found."

"Alex wouldn't be here," said Luther. "He's too smart for that."

"Unless he wants us to think that and stayed here to hit us."

It was a troubling proposition to try to predict the actions of a wolf, Luther thought, especially when he might be functionally insane.

"So you ready?" asked Hampton.

Instead of reading the tea leaves an E-1 agent left behind, they would use some of the tactics the wolf himself had used. Luther was going to hit the streets in order to find him directly.

"I think Alex is on a mission," said Luther. "Whether or not it's inspired by insanity, he has an agenda, and that's how we're going to catch him. We just have to figure out what he's up to."

"Well, we know he took something out of Baltimore," said Hampton. "So if he's here, maybe what he took is what led him to Philly."

"The car we tracked was stolen less than a week ago," said Luther. "If he dumped it here within that time frame, he might not have finished his business here."

"Agreed," said Hampton. "Kilmer is calling in tomorrow morning for progress. Let's have some good news for him."

"We will."

Luther removed his transmitter and started to get out of the Ford.

"Wait. What are you doing?" Hampton demanded.

"If I'm going to get information, I can't look like I'm wired," said Luther.

"No," said Hampton. "Don't take me out of communication. Most of the street people won't even see it."

"Can't take that chance."

"Then I'll send a transmission to your Ion at intervals; just send one back."

"I'll try." Luther got out of the car and walked off.

He roamed the streets of South Philly all night, reacquainting himself with the citizens of inner-city life. He remembered the bizarre combination of fear and excitement you felt as you walked the land, not knowing what lay around the bend.

He was out several hours before he found a source. A pimp, a former prostitute–turned–manager named Sticky B.

Sticky was a tall, good-looking woman of about twenty-five or so. She was of mixed ethnicity, Luther guessed. She had gray-green eyes, a pert little nose that had been broken and never fixed, high cheekbones, and a headful of long black hair that she had tied back with a strand of what appeared to be diamonds. She was dressed in tight black jeans that hugged her generous curves, black stiletto boots, and a black blazer under which she seemed to be wearing nothing. In her right hand she had a cell phone, in the left a gold-capped walking stick.

Her voice was soft and feminine but with an edge to it that suggested that at any moment she might flip on you.

"You wanna talk to me about bid'ness? I can do that," said Sticky, "but anything else smells like a muthafuckin' cop to me."

"If I was a cop, I would have busted you by now," said Luther.

"For what? Being fine?" Sticky B laughed, revealing a gold front tooth that took her pretty face down a few points. "Look, if you with it, we can conversate. If not, roll up yo' dick and push on, nigga. Sticky ain't got no time for cops, faggots, and sexually indecisive muthafuckas."

"Okay," said Luther. "I'm interested in a girl."

"What about it?" said Sticky B.

Luther realized that Sticky B was no fool. She wanted him to solicit her so that she could claim entrapment if he was indeed a cop.

"I'm looking to pay a girl for sex tonight," said Luther. "You satisfied?"

"I am. Shit, I don't watch *Law & Order* for my health, baby. So what you looking for?"

"A white man with a disfigured face."

Sticky B seemed startled for just a second. Then she processed the information, alternating flashing looks of distrust, fear, and deceptive innocence. A life on the street had turned her into an emotional chameleon, and she didn't know which face to choose.

"A girl I can handle," she said, "but the white man I can't help you with. Bad news."

"You know him?" Luther hid his excitement.

"Heard about it, but if you want to know how, you gonna have to pay my girl a premium, you know. And then she'll fill you in."

"How about *you* be my girl tonight?" asked Luther.

Sticky B took on an upset expression, and then she stepped back and threw out her arms. "Do I look like a ho to you? My flat-backin' days are over. I am a playa, a mack, a big, bad-ass daddy with tits." Her face flashed the angry look.

"I can see that, and I don't mean any disrespect. What I meant to say was the information on the white man is valuable, and I don't need to get it from a third party."

Sticky B calmed down. "I see. That's good, because if you got some of this, it would make you go blind anyway." She laughed again and showed Luther the innocent and playful look.

Luther pulled out a hundred-dollar bill and handed it to Sticky B. She took the money, checked it, then pocketed it quickly.

"So what you wanna know?" asked Sticky B.

"The white man with the face, where did you see him?"

"I haven't, but others have. He trying to hide and shit, but, you know, it's only so much hidin' a white man can do 'round here."

"Did you talk to him?" Luther was taking it slowly. He had a feeling that Sticky B might be holding back.

"Oh, hell, no," said Sticky B. "I heard that muthafucka sliced up two of Red's crew. I don't talk to nobody like that. But I do have an idea where he stays."

Sticky B smiled the innocent smile at Luther. He expected her to extort more money out of him. He held out another hundred. She reached for it, and he pulled it back.

"If he isn't there or hasn't been there, or if he got wind of me coming and leaves, I'm coming back to see you."

"My info is always good," said Sticky B.

Luther gave her the money and waited. Sticky B checked the bill and turned back to Luther.

"Can't be too sure these days," she said. "Your man has been traveling between two different places. One is a cheap-ass motel, and the other's a dope house. They don't sell much there, mostly they just use. But they got protection."

"They?" asked Luther

"Red's people."

It was standard mission procedure to have more than one safe house. Luther got the locations and left, repeating his reminder to Sticky B that she would see him again if the information wasn't kosher.

"One last thing," said Luther. "Who's Red?"

"The only bitch in this city that's badder than me."

Luther filed away that last statement and then set out for the drug house. If Alex had a motel room, he would not stay there at night. It would be too dangerous. But at a drug house, there would be people looking out for the cops.

Luther went on foot, armed only with his P99 and a few of Hampton's goodies. He moved carefully through the street, making sure to avoid dangerous-looking men and situations. All his time in E-1 had not robbed him of his street instincts. In fact, he believed that they'd been enhanced by his training.

Finally he came upon the drug house. It was an evil-looking abode, a two-story house that seemed as though it leaned to one side. There was people traffic around the place, and the people were of two kinds: sober-looking young men who cautiously glanced in all directions and tried feebly to hide the fact that they had guns; and lost, dream-walking people stumbling to get inside or away from the place.

Luther watched it from the side of an abandoned house halfway up the street. The night-vision monocular allowed him to see quite clearly the lost souls going in and out of the drug house.

Luther kept watch for more than an hour as the druggies, the dealers, and the young men who served as security engaged each other within their distorted sociology. He waited, remembering what Alex had taught him about patience. Luther could still see Alex at the training facility clad in his black fighting gear, could still hear his voice:

"Sometimes the best way to kill a target is to wait him out. You do nothing but pass the time thinking of the way you will dispatch him. In this regard you wait him to death."

Another hour passed as the night grew deeper, and Luther had the strange feeling that in this desolate place, the night never ended.

And then he saw the wolf.

To anyone else he would have looked like your average deranged street citizen or perhaps a homeless man. But to Luther the straight back, the deliberate moves, the machinelike military gait, and the cautious demeanor gave him away. It was Alex Deavers, his mentor and friend—the wolf.

Alex seemed to be buying something from two men who looked to be dealers. Alex passed bills and took a small plastic bag from one of the men. Luther imagined it had to contain drugs.

Perhaps Alex was in pain, or maybe he'd completely gone off the deep end and was using. Suddenly the exchange turned heated. The men shouted at Alex, and he just watched them and backed away a little, an action that probably seemed weak to them, but Luther knew that Alex needed the distance to attack.

Luther could have gotten a clear shot from where he was, but he had not brought a rifle with him. He might have been able to hit Alex with the silenced P99 he carried, but if he missed, all hell would break loose, and he needed to kill Alex and take the body with him. There could be no loose ends.

Luther had to move. Finding Alex had been good detective work, but it was also part luck, and if Luther didn't engage him this night, he might lose him. And once Alex knew that he was this close, he'd become even harder to find and dispose of.

Luther came out from his hiding place and began to walk toward Alex and the men from the other side of the street. He didn't move too fast, nor did he move too slowly, which might be considered just as suspicious. He set his pace somewhere in the middle, with intent, as anyone might on this street.

Luther was halfway to them when it became clear that the trouble with Alex and the drug dealers was getting worse. One of the dealers pulled a gun and waved it in that juvenile manner dealers display when they're trying to be bad.

It was not a good thing to pull a weapon on an E-1 agent if you did not intend to use it. Luther had only a second to act. Alex would surely attack, and things would get really dangerous on this cracked sidewalk. Luther quickened his pace, pulling his own weapon.

A second after Alex saw the dealer's gun, he kicked it from the man's hand, lifting it into the night. Then Alex hit the man in the throat with a blow that probably bent his windpipe. Another man grabbed Alex and pulled at him. The man ripped Alex's coat, and Luther saw something fall from it. At the same time, a third man took a swing at Alex. Alex pushed himself back against the man holding him and kicked the swinging man in the face with both feet. For a moment Luther was mesmerized by Alex's skill.

Alex threw the man holding him by bending over and dislodging him. The man flew into the air briefly and landed hard on his ass. Luther raised his gun. Alex turned just in time to see Luther.

The two man locked eyes, and for a moment nothing happened. One of the dealers bumped Alex and tried to hit him. Alex used the man's momentum to turn himself from Luther's firing line and put the dealer between them.

Alex took off down the dark street. It was an elegant move that looked planned and not improvised.

The dealer who'd bumped Alex raised a gun and pointed it at Luther, but before he could get off a shot, Luther grabbed the man's arm and bent it. One round fired, and the man released the weapon. Luther grabbed the gun and then hit the dealer on the back of the head with it, dropping him. Then he took off after Alex.

Alex rounded the corner and ran into the street against on-coming traffic. The lights, noise, and cars made him an elusive moving target. Luther pursued, knowing that Alex would run right into a car if it would deter his pursuer. Luckily there was not much traffic, and the few cars that were in the street easily avoided them.

Luther ran steadily, his gun at his side, and he tried not to think about all the memories he had of his friend. He had his duty, which now had to be carried out.

Luther raised his weapon and steadied it as best he could. He was close enough to get a head shot. Shooting Alex in the back of the head seemed cowardly, but he did not have a choice.

Suddenly Alex glanced quickly over his shoulder. Then he turned back and threw both arms up and back in succession. The motion was unnatural and very fast.

The first knife flew by Luther's head, making a thin whizzing sound. Just as his mind registered what the projectile was, he saw the second one coming at him. Luther twisted to avoid it but the second knife slammed into his shoulder. Luther was thrown off his stride by the impact and his attempted maneuver. He toppled to the ground. When he hit the pavement, his gun discharged, making a popping noise.

Luther rolled a few times and then came to a halt. The knife that hit him had fallen out, and he was bleeding. He quickly got up, but it was too late. Alex was gone.

Luther looked around, and it was as if Alex had never been there. In the distance he heard men coming after him. He picked up the knife that had hit him and ran off. He moved to a side street and hid. He couldn't afford another confrontation right now. He was bleeding and would have to get help soon.

The two drug dealers stopped in the middle of the street, yelling, cursing, promising death.

Luther didn't wait around. There was nothing else to be done here. He was about to move off when he saw something that made him stop. One of the men was holding a small green card. Luther recognized it as an R-card, a sophisticated data and information card. That's what had fallen out of Alex's coat during the fight. The man with the card looked at it and said something to his friend.

Luther was injured, but he had to get that card from the dealers now. If they escaped, they might destroy it.

The dealers, tired of trash talk, put away their weapons and walked off.

Luther ran from his hiding place toward the men. It was the one on his left who had the green card. Luther ran to the man on his right and hit him hard in the kidneys, then spun and swept the legs of the man with the card out from under him. The man fell hard. Luther finished the first man with a blow to the head.

He pulled his gun and put it into the face of the second man. "The green card. Give it to me."

The man handed Luther the card.

"The man you got this from, the white man, where did he get it?"

"I don't know, man!" said the dealer fearfully.

"How long did he have it?" asked Luther.

"I don't know! He dropped it when we was fightin'. First time I ever seen it."

Luther felt the sting of his wound. He stepped over the fallen man and ran off.

When Luther got back to the safe house, Hampton dressed his wound, which was pretty nasty. He'd lost a lot of blood, and his pride was hurt as well. Luther had underestimated Alex, but they had surprised him by finding him so quickly, and he'd made a mistake. Luther had the card.

"So he hit you with a knife, running blind?" asked Hampton as he cleaned out the gash.

"Yes," said Luther. "He took a quick look to make sure I was right behind him; then he tossed them over his shoulder."

"Man, he's good."

"Tell me about it," said Luther.

"So he had an R-card," said Hampton. "Let's hope the wolf never got a chance to access it. Maybe we can beat him to the information on it."

Luther noticed that Hampton refused to use Alex's name and always referred to him as "the wolf" or "him," anything but a human appellation. In Hampton's mind Alex was no longer a person. He was only the target of the mission.

If I were you, I'd kill my TWA.

Against his will, Luther's training brought back Alex's voice. Hampton had taken a big step shooting the man in Baltimore. It was justified to some extent, but out of character nonetheless. Luther put this thought away. He would not let Alex's mind game cloud his judgment.

"You know, the R-card is outdated technology," said Hampton. "I thought they were all recalled years ago. I'll have to use an adapter for it. Luckily, I'm always prepared."

"Alex must've gotten the R-card from some hiding place. He's collecting information, old information, for some reason. We need to access that card."

Hampton took out a little box that looked like a CD jewel case and plugged it in to his computer.

"Dammit," said Hampton. "It's been erased."

"Erased?" asked Luther. "Is there anything you can do?"

"I don't know," said Hampton. "I'll need to access the mainframe on a hard line. I'll need a reconstruction program. R-cards have a rudimentary encryption, but if we don't repair it just right, we'll get nothing. It's gonna take a while."

"Work all night," said Luther. "I'll stay up and stand watch at the safe house."

"Why?" asked Hampton.

"Because either Alex has a head start on us or he's watching right now, planning to get that card back. Since we don't know which . . ."

"We assume the worst," said Hampton.

Luther took them back to a hard line at the safe house. He stood guard as Hampton went about the task of restoring the information on the R-card. Luther watched the screen as the program slowly popped up codes and data at a snail's pace. By daybreak Hampton had succeeded.

The laptop's screen gave latitude and longitude readings and bore the code "AI" in the upper right corner.

" 'AI,' " Hampton muttered. "That's England."

"England?" asked Luther.

"AI stands for Angel Isle. It's an old agency term for Great Britain," said Hampton.

"Why would a British R-card be used?" said Luther.

"I don't know," said Hampton. "Best guess is whoever used it didn't want anyone in this country to know what he was doing. R-cards were always accounted for by E-1, as I recall."

"So he had time to erase it, but why not just destroy it?" Luther wondered. "Surely Alex knows that we have the technology to repair the card and reassemble the data on it. And if that's the case, then why erase it in the first place?"

"This guy's gonna give me a headache," said Hampton. "You ever think about the fact that we're trying to figure out the mind of a man who might be insane?"

"Yes. That means we're thinking like crazy men," said Luther.

"Uh-huh. And is that a good thing?" asked Hampton.

"Right now it's all we've got," said Luther.

"Okay, so let's say he wanted us to find the card. That means the wolf obviously wanted us to follow him again."

"Yes, but he didn't expect us to find him at that drug house," said Luther. "Maybe he was on his way somewhere to leave the card for us so that we'd find it."

"But that still doesn't explain why he erased it," said Hampton. "Unless—"

"He just wanted to slow us down," said Luther. "Part of getting this chase thing to work means that Alex has to stay ahead of us, right?"

"Right," said Hampton. "He'd know that a lengthy reconstruction on the card would slow us down. I mean, we wouldn't know where to go until we got the intel from the card."

Hampton ran the latitude and longitude numbers through a mapping program.

Luther looked at the screen and smiled a little. Alex was not being cagey this time around. He was going to a specific place.

Harlem

They'd lost valuable time repairing the R-card, and so they drove all day to reach New York. By afternoon they were parked across from an office building in Harlem. It was in a nice area of the city, a far cry from the others they'd been to, but Harlem was a hard neighborhood that had seen worse days.

"Let's hope we're getting there first," said Luther.

"The E-1 mainframe said that the R-card was twenty years old," said Hampton. "This building has been refurbished within the last three years. It was a government building that housed nonlethal federal agencies. It was also a drop point for the CIA. Now it's an office building."

"A drop point like the VA in Baltimore," said Luther.

"Which cover are you using?"

"FBI," said Luther.

"Try not to get killed," said Hampton.

"What happened to 'Don't kill anybody'?" asked Luther.

"After what the wolf did, I think it's time for a change."

Luther got out of the truck and moved toward the building. He walked inside and went straight to security. He showed his badge and waited while they called it in. His cover was verified, and Luther was led to the basement utility room.

"They're sure sending a lot of feds here today," said the guard, a thin black man of fifty.

"What other men have been here?" asked Luther casually. He didn't want to alarm the guard.

"Some guy from OSHA. Said he was expecting more men."

"When did he get here?"

"An hour ago," said the guard. "He was wearing one of them safety masks."

"When did he leave?" asked Luther.

"I didn't see him go," said the guard.

Luther took off running.

"He was here!" said Luther to Hampton. "Call it in!"

"The drop point is in the east wall, at the base," said Hampton. He was looking a schematic of the building on his computer.

Luther got to the basement door and stopped. He opened the door quietly and went inside, his gun out, locking the door behind him so the guard couldn't follow. The room was bright and filled with electrical equipment and supplies. At the far end was a massive heating unit.

"I'm in," said Luther.

He took a small step forward. The room was basically a big square. The walls were slate gray, and the place smelled faintly of mold and chemicals.

Luther moved slowly. If Alex was here, he still had the element of surprise.

"Director patching in," said Hampton quietly.

"Is it Deavers?" asked Kilmer on the line.

"Haven't seen him yet," said Luther. "A lot of hiding places in this basement."

Luther went in farther. He made sure to move in circles so that no one one could maneuver behind him.

"Don't let him get away this time," said Kilmer.

Luther's eyes narrowed at this, but he kept moving. He went toward the eastern wall, checked the baseboard, and was disappointed to see that part of it had been pried open. There was nothing behind it.

"Shit," said Luther, "Alex has been here. Repeat, he's been here and—"

Luther saw a door. He moved to it, his gun held out in front. He went to the back of the heating unit, where shadows crept into the bright room. When he got there, he saw a door leading up to the street. It was open.

"He's gone," said Luther.

"Get after him," said Kilmer. "He can't have gone far."

"Shall I coordinate the locals?" asked Hampton.

"That might be a good—" Kilmer began.

"Wait." Luther cut him off. "There's something wrong here."

He'd noticed that the heating unit had been tampered with. A metal pipe was connected to the front gauges. These in turn were covered in thick layers of duct tape. The pipe ran from the gauges to the back of the heating unit.

Luther described the setup to Hampton and Kilmer.

"Can you find the model number?" asked Hampton.

Luther located it at the front of the unit on one of its many panels. He gave it to Hampton, then immediately heard Hampton tapping away at his laptop. There was a brief silence, and then Luther heard him sigh.

"We got a problem," said Hampton.

"Forget it," said Kilmer. "You two go after Deavers right now."

"Sir, I think he's rigged a toxic bomb," said Hampton. "That unit is a Model TLX from Newton Heating. It's computerized. The wolf may have rigged the exhaust to heat up the monitoring gauges. When that happens, the unit will automatically go into cooldown mode by mixing an inhibited glycol-based coolant. This is okay if the unit is actually overheating."

"And if not?" asked Luther, suddenly alarmed.

"It will emit a toxic gas that can cause brain damage or kill. Here's the best part: The gas is almost totally odorless."

"I'm on it," said Luther, and he began to peel away the duct tape slowly.

"No," said Kilmer. "Get out of there. Deavers is making time on you."

"There are innocent people in this building, sir," said Luther.

"The locals can handle it," said Kilmer.

"We don't know if there's enough time," Luther insisted.

"Acquiring Deavers is your priority. Out of the building—now!"

"Negative, sir," said Luther. "We have a dangerous situation, and it is not E-1 procedure to—"

"Don't quote the rules to me," said Kilmer. "I wrote them! Agent Hampton . . ."

Luther got to the bottom of the tape. He saw the gauges intact. There was nothing connecting the gauges and the pipe. It was a decoy. But on the thick-gauge glass was something he hadn't expected.

A message. It was on a small piece of paper taped to the glass.

"The unit is uncompromised," said Luther.

"Go. Now." Kilmer hung up the line.

Luther took the message and left the building. He walked quietly through the lobby, rendezvoused outside with Hampton, and they drove off.

They did a standard sweep of the area and listened as the locals were given a general description of Alex Deavers. Luther told Hampton the text of Alex's message. They knew they'd be moving on, but at Kilmer's insistence they searched the rest of the night. Again Alex proved elusive.

"Kilmer wanted me to let the unit disperse the gas," said Luther later on as they sat in the airport terminal.

They'd had to move both hell and high water to get their weapons through. They were taking a charter plane out, and Luther felt a sense of dread about where they were going.

"And he was serious," said Hampton. "All he wants is the wolf."

The director was willing to sacrifice the lives of hundreds of people to catch Alex, Luther thought. That was not the way of E-1, even for a wolf. Alex wanted Luther to know that Kilmer for some reason was willing to let innocents die in order to get him, subvert the rules to get to him. Luther realized that taking any message from a wolf was dangerous, especially after the mayhem Alex had visited upon other agents in the field. But Luther's instinct was calling to him now and he could not deny it.

Something was not right.

". . . *That information, too.*"

What did Alex know that would make Kilmer endanger innocent people? Luther decided that he would not share his suspicions with anyone, not even Hampton, at this point.

". . . *I'd kill my TWA.*"

When Kilmer had gotten angry, he'd called upon Hampton and then stopped when Luther announced that the device was harmless. What had Kilmer been planning to ask Hampton to do? he wondered.

Luther and Hampton walked from the terminal to the charter plane on the tarmac. Luther tried to ease the trouble he felt swirling in his head. He pushed these thoughts aside and was left with only Alex's daunting message:

"*Go home.*"

To Luther's hometown, Detroit.

ADVERSARY GAME

An operative may use the personal contacts of a
target against him if necessary to complete a
mission. The use of such contacts may include
lethal action.

—E-1 Operations Mission Manual, Rule 35

Cass Corridor

They'd landed at Metro Airport and picked up a new vehicle, another Ford Explorer. A little smile worked its way across Luther's face. Home. After ten years he was back home. Luther sped down I-94 as the sun was setting. They'd flown into Detroit from New York, hoping to make up some time on Alex. The wolf would not use the airport because of security, but they could.

"Detroit," said Hampton. "I spent a week here one night."

"You didn't like it?" asked Luther.

"No. It has a weird vibe, and everybody seems so separated. Haven't you people learned to get along yet?"

"Apparently not," said Luther.

Luther and Kilmer had had a conversation after the bomb incident in New York. Kilmer had been intense before, but during their conversation he was back to his usual unreadable self.

Luther didn't tell him he suspected that the wolf was trying to communicate with him through the mission. What he did tell him was that Alex had left a clue that led them to Detroit. Kilmer had been silent about this and inquired no further. If Luther knew the director, Kilmer was thinking about replacing him on the mission. He had to get to Alex before Kilmer made that decision.

Luther took the Lodge Freeway to Warren, then exited and drove to Cass Avenue, a place notorious for criminal activities. Although the area was making a comeback, many parts of it still resembled a ghost town, a place where people didn't go unless they were on their way to the grave. This was a good place to start hunting for Alex.

Luther looked out at the bleakness of the neighborhood and remembered how he had been told by his parents never to come here. "People die there," his mother had said.

"Alex knows I'm from Detroit," said Luther. "He brought me here intentionally."

"Rule 35?" asked Hampton.

Luther remembered E-1 Rule 35, the personal-contact rule. It allowed an agent to use the personal contacts of a target if it would help complete his mission. Rule 35's wording clearly set it forth as a last-ditch measure, but Luther was certain that Alex would consider whatever mission he was on critical and invoke the rule against him.

"I imagine so," said Luther.

They drove off toward the east side. He knew that Alex was holed up somewhere in the poorest part of the city. He was sorry to say that in his hometown, that could be many places.

After nightfall Luther and Hampton nestled themselves into the safe house just off the east side of the city. It was a nice two-bedroom home in a forgettable neighborhood.

When Luther's Ion rang, he answered it, making sure that the proper code was being received.

"Hello," he said.

"What happened in New York can never happen again," said Kilmer flatly, with a finality that was a little frightening.

"Yes, sir," said Luther. He put the phone on speaker. "He's led me to my hometown."

"I know," said Kilmer with a measured concern. "I thought about bringing you in for that reason." Luther detected an edge in the director's voice. After Luther's defiance in New York, Kilmer wanted Luther to remember that he had the power to end this mission.

"Alex obviously wants to weaken your position on this," said Kilmer.

"I agree, sir," said Hampton. "So far the wolf has been operating as if he's got a plan. Coming here is part of it."

"I haven't been home in over ten years," said Luther. "No one's looking for me."

"Not the point, and you know it," said Kilmer. "The presence of personal contacts weakens you."

"Yes, sir," said Luther. As usual, Kilmer was right.

"You may request to remove yourself, if you wish," said Kilmer calmly.

"No, sir," said Luther.

"Acknowledged," said Kilmer.

"Sir," said Luther, wanting to get past this inquiry, "we believe that Alex is collecting information in each of the cities he's been in. We don't know what this info is, but he's risking his life for it."

"I was afraid of that," said Kilmer. "Deavers is obviously under the impression that he's acting on some order. Whatever he's collecting, I want you to secure it after he's neutralized."

"Yes, sir," said Luther and Hampton, almost as one.

"I think the wolf is functionally insane, sir," said Hampton, "retaining all his practical faculties but living in a state of delusion."

"Interesting," said Kilmer. "Is there anything else?"

"No, sir," said Luther, with Hampton echoing.

"Are you sure?"

Luther and Hampton were mildly shocked. Kilmer almost never repeated himself.

"Yes, sir, I'm sure," said Luther.

Kilmer terminated the call. It was by far the strangest conversation Luther had ever had with the director.

"If I didn't know any better, I'd think Kilmer was worried about something," said Hampton.

"He is," said Luther. "The question is, what? Kilmer has always been cool when it comes to missions. Remember when they blew that hit in Salvador and it caused a little three-day civil war? He was as calm as could be, even as he ordered the deaths of ten men."

Luther ended this line of thinking out loud, but inside he was thinking that Kilmer seemed very afraid of something on this mission, and given the history of E-1, it had to be something terrible.

Hampton hooked his mobile informational unit to the phone line, which in turn was hooked to a transmission booster. After working a few minutes, he was into E-1's database. He needed to do some research. Maybe he'd find something that would help them in locating their prey.

"I'm looking at crime stats," said Hampton. "There are a lot of bad sectors in Detroit. But this one here, adjacent to downtown, seems to be one of the worst."

"Let's go out and find him," said Luther. "Get a lock on the area, and let's canvass it."

"It's gonna be a big area," said Hampton.

"We're big men," said Luther, and he smiled at his friend.

"You want me, a little white dude, to go out asking questions in a black neighborhood?"

"Yes, and don't kill anybody," said Luther.

Luther got ready to hit the streets, dressing in jeans, an old hooded sweatshirt, and sneakers. He glanced at himself in the mirror. He was looking as he had long ago, before he left. Which man was he, the international government assassin or the home-boy who'd come home at last?

He checked Hampton's outfit. He was similarly dressed down. Luther approved, then watched as Hampton loaded the Baby Eagle and stuck it into his waistband.

They both set out and then split up after Hampton acquired his own vehicle from the local CIA field office. Luther drove the Ford into the city. His heart sank at the sight of Tiger Stadium abandoned and then soared when he saw the new Comerica Park with its fierce stone tigers chewing baseballs.

The Fox Theatre looked as it had in days of old, the Detroit Opera House was beautifully restored, and Ford Field, a spectac-ular state-of-the-art indoor football stadium, was open for business and boasted a sign heralding a coming Super Bowl.

Luther drove to the near east side, just a few miles from down-town, and parked. He then set off on foot. There were many bad areas in the city, but this was perhaps the worst. In most big cities, the downtown area had the poor relations of prosperity close by.

Luther combed the neighborhood, asking every shady character he saw about a disfigured white man who might be spreading money around. He got many offers to buy drugs and one offer for sex, but no information. Still, he was sure the news would spread that he was looking for Alex and that it would get back to him.

"Yo, yo, yo," said a dark, thin man to Luther as he was preparing to call it a day. "I got what you need, brutha."

Luther surveyed the man. He had dyed-blond hair, which only made his dark skin look darker. He was wearing a Pistons warm-up jacket and black jeans.

"What you got?" asked Luther, coming closer.

"You name it," said the man. "Ask anybody. Sharpie is the man on the street. Like I always say, if you want it, Sharpie can get it for ya."

Luther had to suppress a smile. A criminal with a marketing plan and a motto struck him funny.

"I'm looking for a man," said Luther.

"Damn," said Sharpie. "You don't look like the type for that. Okay, cool, I know this young boy over on—"

"Not like that," said Luther. "The man I'm looking for owes me money on a deal, and I need to find him."

"Black or white?"

"White."

"Cop or cool?"

"He's not a cop. He's tall and has some old wounds on his face. And you do not want to fuck with him."

Sharpie looked into the air, thinking. He scratched his long chin and rubbed his eye once. "Can't say I've heard anything about a man like that, but I'll keep an ear open for you. So you sure you don't want anything? I got ecstasy, weed, and ludes— shit, I even got some blue boys. It's a cooled-out version of that shit they used to call cold medina."

"No thanks," said Luther.

"Well, damn," said Sharpie. "You gotta be the straightest muthafucka in Detroit."

"Just tryin' to get my money. Who's the man on the street these days?"

"Shit, that could be a lot of people," said Sharpie, looking a little disappointed that he wasn't going to make some kind of sale. "Lynch, Crazy-G, Pitch Black, Nappy, Brenda Cream—I hate that bitch—and there's this new boy they all call Damn!"

"Who's the smartest of those men?"

"They all dumb-asses, if you ask me. Be dead inside a year and replaced by niggas just like 'em. Except Brenda and Nappy. They pretty smart."

It had occurred to Luther that for Alex to operate in Detroit, he would have to make a street ally. He could just kill anyone who got in his way, but in the end a white man in this town would be taken out by sheer numbers if he tried to maintain power like that. And Alex would not assume leadership of a criminal enterprise. It was too dangerous. He needed someone who was smart and resourceful, essentially a subagent.

"What's Brenda into?" asked Luther, taking the least obvious one first.

"That bitch? Man, she into everything. Drugs, robbery, carjackin'. That female even put her own cousin to work as a ho."

"What about Nappy?"

"Well, he's a class act as they go. He's older, been in the joint and lived to tell. He tries to run a little newspaper, but everybody knows what his real bid'ness is, you know? He's a smart nigga, for real, but I wouldn't mess with him. Folks got a funny-ass way of just disappearin' around him."

That was his man, thought Luther. This Nappy sounded like just the right fit for a domestic urban mission. Hell, from the sound of it, Luther wished he'd found Nappy first. Alex would never take on a woman, even if she was as tough as Brenda sounded.

"Thanks. I'm gonna be in touch with you." Luther handed Sharpie some money and squeezed his hand hard to let him know that they now had a relationship.

"Cool," said Sharpie, looking happier that his talk had just become profitable. "What's your name?"

"Ain't got one right now, and you can't find me. I'll find you."

Luther walked off and got the feeling that Sharpie was boring a hole into the back of his head. He'd planted many seeds in the street community tonight. When Alex heard that someone was looking for him, he'd react. Luther just hoped it wouldn't be a reaction with fatal consequences.

Nappy and Jewel

Tevin knew that someone was going to die. No reason to be doing something like this, he thought. There were bad things in the city, terrible things, and God knows he'd seen and caused a lot of them, but this, this was just *wrong*. Violence was a medium of exchange on the street, like money. You gave up the mayhem, and in return an enemy was gone or a treasure won. But violence for no reason was foolish if not crazy, and that was what they were doing this day. They were giving away money. He'd made it a long time on the street, and one of the reasons he had was that he didn't do this kind of shit.

Tevin Williams stood in the middle of the living room of a vacant house on the east side of Detroit. He and his partner were waiting for their boss, and he was getting impatient.

"I don't get this," Tevin said to Jimon, a thick-necked thug he rode with these days. "Why he wanna do some shit like that?"

"Man say we gotta," said Jimon, chomping on a hamburger he'd just bought from Burger King. He ate it with an abandon that suggested that it was his last meal, a common trait among those who aren't sure whether any meal will be their last. Jimon was not too bright, but he was tough, big, and ruthless—all good qualities on the street.

"Yo, here come the man," said Tevin. He looked out the dirty window.

The black car rolled smoothly down the street, the sun gleaming off its polished hood, throwing light into the air. It was a classic, a 1972 Buick Electra 225, known in the inner city as a Deuce and a Quarter. It rode on wide, low-profile tires and looked as though its chrome had been buffed just seconds earlier. It was a bad-ass ride, from its modified fins to its evil, smiling grille.

The door of the Buick opened, and out stepped a tall, angular man in his forties. He stood about six foot two and seemed to unfold as he got out of the car, rising to his full height. He was dressed in a long black coat that covered a crisp, spotless white shirt and jeans, his standard uniform. To a passerby he would have appeared to be a man on some kind of mission—an undercover cop, a street soldier, a guardian against some unseen enemy. He had a menace about him, a look that let anyone know he was not to be dismissed as ordinary.

Nappy jingled his keys in his left hand and shut the door to the Buick. His hands were large, with long, knobby fingers and manicured nails. He wore no jewelry save a gold band on his left index finger. His face was angular like the rest of him, spare and tight. His eyes were deep set, and the shadows from his brow made them seem black. They were actually light brown, and they held within them the hardness and horror of a lifetime on the street. His goatee, trimmed to perfection, completed his intimidating appearance, which was crowned by a shining bald head.

Nappy walked into the house. He went past the two men without saying a word and turned his back on them.

The three men stood unmoving for a while. Tevin and Jimon knew not to speak first to their boss. He sometimes disliked that. Fear filled the room. Their employer and their occupation made Tevin and Jimon worry about injury and death. Tevin was already starting to sweat.

"I suppose you've been wondering about your mission of last night, why I'd ask you to do something like that," Nappy said in a voice that was measured and precise.

"Naw, Nappy, we wasn't," said Jimon too quickly.

"I was talking to Tevin," said Nappy. "I know you don't question me, Jimon, correct?"

"No, sir," said Jimon immediately.

"Tevin?" asked Nappy. "Don't you think this is some bullshit?"

Tevin swallowed hard and then opened his mouth to speak. Beside him Jimon had unconsciously taken a step back.

Tevin considered his answer carefully. Nappy never asked a question that he didn't already know the answer to. It was never good to try to lie your way around him.

"Yes," said Tevin. "It ain't about business, you know." Tevin's last words almost ran out of breath, as if he were forcing them out past his fear.

Nappy waited a moment, a long moment—an eternity, it seemed to the two men behind him.

"You're right," said Nappy, still with his back turned. "It's some bullshit, but it does have a purpose . . . to me. Unfortunately, my purpose provides that I can't have anyone know what we did last night. I can't afford to have two weak-ass men with knowledge of it. So I can't let the two of you leave here alive."

For a moment Jimon and Tevin just stood there as the words hit their ears, a heavy batch of sound. Nappy didn't move. He stood resolute in what he had just said, a dark statue of confidence.

Tevin pulled his gun.

"Not today, muthafucka," said Tevin. He raised the gun at Nappy's back and held it steady.

"What the fuck?" said Jimon, alarm in his voice.

"You heard what he said!" said Tevin. "He brought us here to kill us!"

"Nigga, stop trippin'," said Jimon. "Why would he do that and turn his back on us like that? We could just shoot him. He's testing us, and your dumb ass failed."

"Bullshit," said Tevin. "He ain't playin'. He don't ever bullshit about canceling somebody. No, he for real, but he the one who ain't leaving this house." Tevin cocked the weapon.

Jimon's feeble mind tried to grasp the situation he was in. Nappy was the man, but Tevin did have a point. Nappy never kidded about murder. But if this was one of his tests, it was just the kind Nappy would give. When you passed one of Nappy's tests, there were often great rewards—money, power, women. Jimon was not about to let Tevin's foolishness keep him from those riches.

Jimon pulled his gun and then put it to Tevin's head.

"What the hell you doin', fool?" asked Tevin.

"Gimme yo' gun," said Jimon. "I got it, boss," he said to Nappy. "It's cool."

"Don't be stupid," said Tevin. "He's—"

"Not gonna ask you again," said Jimon, pressing the gun harder into Tevin's temple.

Tevin dropped his arm a little, as if to hand over the weapon, then quickly swung his weapon back up and around toward Jimon's head. Jimon saw Tevin's arm go up, and immediately he fired. The shot blew into Tevin's head. Tevin jerked and sent off a shot that caught Jimon in the neck, severing his jugular. Both men fell to the floor, dropping their respective weapons. Tevin didn't move. He was dead. The bullet had torn through his brain, and he was gone before he hit the cracked floor.

Jimon was hit but still alive. He squirmed and wiggled as he tried to stop the blood that rushed out of the wound between his clasped fingers.

Nappy turned and surveyed the destruction. He thought that Jimon, being the brute he was, would shoot Tevin, and then Nappy in turn would take Jimon out himself. But it seemed fate had another plan. This was even better, Nappy thought. The fact that they'd killed each other made him guilt-free in two deaths.

Nappy walked over and knelt next to Jimon, careful not to step in the blood.

"Help," Jimon managed to say, blood spurting from his mouth. His voice was already weak. He was slipping away.

"Loyalty is a good quality," said Nappy. "But it's not everything a man needs to survive."

Nappy got up and strolled out of the house. Behind him he heard Jimon struggle and choke until he fell silent.

Nappy walked into the hazy sunshine of the day and headed toward the Buick. He got into the car and settled into the plush new leather seats he'd installed. He bought new seats every two years for the vintage car. The smell of African incense filled the interior. He started the car, and the big V-8 roared to life. Nappy pulled away from the little house, rolling down the dismal street.

He didn't worry about the gunfire. In this neighborhood no one would call the police, and even if they did, what had he really

just done? No crime in talking two men to death. That would be
a great case, he thought. Let's see the system try to convict him of
that.

Nappy pushed a button on his sound system and Al Green
came on singing "Let's Stay Together."

Chokwe Muhammad had gotten his nickname in the hospital
the night he was born. The thick black hair he'd been born with
was tightly wound into curls that separated nicely on his head.
They looked like kinks, or naps, as they say. His father had called
him Nappy as a joke, and the name stuck.

Nappy hid his criminal activities by starting an organization called Black Truth that published a newspaper he dubbed
The Radical. It was his way of merging his past and his future.
Black Truth was his way of remembering his father, a former
sixties radical, and it provided an excellent cover for his business.

Black Truth was popular in the neighborhoods. It was regularly
raided by the police and had been put on the FBI's subversive list,
which only made him proud.

Nappy reasoned that his criminal activities were just a re-
source. The black man had been left the drug trade as the only
means of support for his efforts.

Nappy's Black Truth was dedicated to exposing government
conspiracies and oppression. He was pleased to learn that there
were many people like him in the country who questioned the
essence of government purity.

Nappy turned down a residential street, parked, and approached his mother's house. He'd been planning to go to his
office but remembered that he had not made his weekly check on
his family.

He walked up to the little house on Maine. Unlike the other houses on the block, this one was pretty. It was nestled between a vacant lot and another house that looked like something had fallen on it. There was prosperity in this little home.

Nappy climbed the steps and pressed the doorbell. The door opened, and an old black woman peered out. She was sixty or so and very round. She had a headful of gray hair that was cut into a neat Afro. She looked at Nappy from behind thick glasses, her face hard and unsmiling.

"You got a gun?" asked the woman.

"Why do we gotta go through this every time?" said Nappy. "I ain't giving up my—"

The door slammed in Nappy's face, and he heard the sound of receding footsteps and the old woman's curses.

"Rita!" yelled Nappy. "Open this damned door!"

A moment passed, and Nappy hissed, cursing to himself about the old woman. Soon he heard approaching footsteps, accompanied by Rita's complaining voice.

The door opened, this time by another woman. She was about the same age as the other, but much thinner and sporting black-and-gray dreadlocks. She smiled at Nappy.

"I'm gon' kill her, Mama," said Nappy. "I swear."

He hated Rita, but she was his mother's best friend and had nursed her through an illness some years back. Rita was a strong and very religious woman who now shared the home with his mother, serving as cook, maid, and protector. She didn't like Nappy for very obvious reasons.

"No threats in my house," said Tawanna Muhammad, Nappy's mother. "Come on in."

A half hour later, they were sitting at the kitchen table eating.

Nappy wasn't hungry, but when your mother wanted to feed you, you didn't dare say no.

He sat with his mother and his niece Jewel, a young girl of sixteen. She was dark brown, with glowing skin and big brown eyes that pierced your heart even from a distance. She was a magnificent young woman, and he was determined not to let the city snuff out her light.

After his sister died leaving young Jewel, Nappy had begged his mother to move the child out of Detroit, but Tawanna didn't want to leave the city. And so Nappy had to settle for the protection he bought with fear.

After dinner Rita and Tawanna left. As soon as they were gone, Nappy spoke to his niece.

"I do a lot of things I'm not proud of, but in the end I'm trying to be a good man. You got to remember that." He thought about his action in Dearborn and the trouble that was to come. And then Nappy handed Jewel a wad of cash under the table. "Don't let Mama or Rita know you got that."

"I never do," said Jewel.

Nappy's concern about his niece was more than paternal. One day Jewel would assume his position and carry on his work at *The Radical*, but when she did, the paper would be legitimate. He'd make it so with the money he'd been saving and the big stories he was getting from Wolf.

He was too smart to think he'd ever see the dream turn into reality himself. He was too old and too tainted. He'd give Jewel the dream, and he'd share it through her. By the time she got out of college, he'd be giving her the *New York Times* of alternative newspapers.

Nappy said good-bye to his mother. He offered her money, and she said no, insisting that she had enough for right now. He looked outside and found the thugs across the street gone, out for their night's work. He worried about his family living here in the danger of this lost place. But his mother was still a tough old bird, and she was *not* going anywhere.

Nappy kissed his niece good-bye in the doorway, then got into his car and rode off.

He traveled the city for a while checking on his street dealers and making sure the money was flowing the right way. Business was good, and so he eagerly headed off to his place of business to close the deal on the day's activities in Dearborn.

Nappy drove the Buick onto Linwood Avenue and was soon in front of the offices of Black Truth. The red, black, and green sign proclaimed the organization to be THE LIGHT OF THE PEOPLE. Armed guards kept watch on the place.

The Black Truth offices occupied almost the entire block, sharing shared space with a soul-food joint and a small printing company that Nappy also owned part of.

He walked inside, not lingering with his people. Ten workers buzzed about the office. Nappy's criminal organization was much bigger, but the street dealers were not allowed to come close to this place. The FBI would have liked nothing better than to catch him on another drug charge.

Nappy entered the premises slowly and deliberately, as he always did. He didn't want anyone to think he was in a hurry or in any way different from how he was on any other day. What he, Tevin, and Jimon had done would bring the cops, and when they and the FBI came, they wouldn't hear anything incriminating from anyone. That was, if they came at all. Nappy never underestimated their stupidity.

He walked down the hallway to his office, located in the back of the building. The lights were low, and the sounds from the outer office faded. Soon all he heard was the muted noises from the street outside.

Inside his office Nappy immediately sensed a presence. He scanned the place, and his eyes settled on a figure nestled in the far corner. The man was half turned away from him. Nappy approached the man slowly, as he always did. Sudden moves were not healthy in this man's presence. Nappy didn't ask the man how he'd gotten in or how he'd evaded detection by his staff. He knew by now that this man had his ways, that he was like a ghost when he had to be.

"Is it done?" asked the man in his scratchy, tortured voice.

"Yes," said Nappy.

"And your operatives?"

"Just like you said . . . what was it called?"

"Backwashed," said the man, who got to his feet. He stood straight at attention and turned. Nappy was always aware of the grace and elegance of his movements. It was one of the first things he'd noticed about him when they met.

"Excellent," said the man. "I have your payment."

The man reached into his pocket and removed an envelope, tossing it to Nappy. Inside, Nappy found a copy of a secret FBI plan to detain inner-city populations in case of domestic terrorism. The containment plan was clearly aimed at African-Americans.

The man come toward Nappy. Light from the dimmed overhead lamps moved over him, cutting his face into sections of shadow and light as he approached, and soon Nappy looked directly into the mangled face of Alex Deavers.

"Things will happen swiftly now," said Deavers.

"What things?" asked Nappy.

"The government will react, and the community will fall into its politically correct responses. So we must be quick with phase two."

"It's already begun," said Nappy. "I got a nice little crew of boys who are gonna go into the Arab neighborhoods and raise a little hell."

Deavers didn't respond. He went to the window and looked out. In the back of the building, he saw Nappy's nameplate. His face contorted. No one could tell, but he was smiling. It was ironic humor indeed, he thought. The Buick Electra's nickname was a Deuce and a Quarter, which stood for the car's number, 225, an ominous integer that only Alex understood.

"Nice ride," he said.

At 4:35 P.M. in Dearborn, a fire started in the cellar of an Arab-American community center. The incendiary device was crude, but effective enough to set off a fire that engulfed the building and sent two people to the emergency room.

Cries of anti-Arab violence were immediately sounded. The FBI was called in, and the city was placed on a high terrorism alert.

•

Amreeka

The specters moved with a fierce quickness in the early hours of the morning. It was still very dark outside, and they took advantage of that fact by wearing dark clothes. Invisible and lethal, they carried the seeds of death in their minds.

They approached the dwellings of their enemies and struck with precision and power. They left their curse on homes, schools, and businesses. They smashed cars and blighted billboards. They even put their mark on busy intersections for all to see. They had power, and they wanted everyone to know it.

The vandals wreaked havoc and spread hatred that night. They had been well paid by a man who was of Middle Eastern extraction and who seemed not to care that he was harming his own people. This man in turn was paid by a white man who had known criminal ties. The white man had been paid by another white man, a friend who trafficked in inner-city drugs. And that man had been given his instructions by one of Nappy's best lieutenants.

The specters finished their work and moved on. The city lay behind them, bearing the mark of their anger and nurturing the seeds of rising discontent.

Dearborn, Michigan, a suburb of Detroit, is home to the largest Arab population outside the Middle East. There are some three hundred thousand and counting.

The first immigrants arrived in the 1870s. They were from the Ottoman province of Syria, an area that would become known as Lebanon. Their numbers swelled as they brought their relatives from overseas to the land they called "Amreeka." They flooded in: the Lebanese, Yemenites, Syrians, Palestinians, Egyptians, Iraqi Shia, and Chaldeans. They came in droves, populating the city of Henry Ford's birth and giving rise to an ethnic minority that has defied assimilation and built a political and economic power base.

Alex Deavers had been aware of this for many years through E-1. In fact, he had put together the first national database on Arab-Americans after the initial terror attacks on soldiers during the Carter administration. He was an expert in the area and was happily surprised to find that the CIA and E-1 had chosen this city in which to hide their dirtiest secret.

Alex stood near Tiger Stadium. It was closed down now and abandoned, a ghost of itself. Alex loved baseball and lamented the new stadiums and their corporate sponsors. Who wanted to watch the almost spiritual game of baseball in a park named after a god-damned financial institution?

Alex tilted his hat a little as a car passed by. There were homeless men about, and he couldn't help but think of them as scavengers and the stadium a dead animal. He got into another car and drove away, certain that this would be a great day in his quest.

An hour later a parking-lot attendant called the city's impound service to take away a car for which he had no key or parking receipt. The car had been sitting all day in his lot, close to the McNamara Federal Building. When the tow-truck operator popped the lock on the car, he discovered thick wires running from the steering panel into the backseat.

Within minutes the fire department and four agencies of law enforcement, local and federal, were on the scene. The city bomb squad traced the thick wires and successfully removed them from the car's full gas tank.

In less than an hour, the place was a full-blown police crime scene and media circus. Stories about the vandals Alex had sent to Dearborn to deface certain areas with anti-Arab slurs were all over the news. Everyone was waving U.S. flags and copies of the Constitution. The victimization process was well under way, he thought. Today the media would report that someone had tried to strike back.

The attempted attack near a federal facility was seen as retaliation. The antiterrorism unit in Detroit would be mobilized, and by tomorrow the city would be placed on its highest level of alert ever.

Now more local and federal police power would be shifted to protect public buildings and concerns. Correspondingly, they would decrease manpower in other areas. This was what Alex had been waiting for.

Nappy and his minions had done a good job in Dearborn. The armies would now be set against each other, and they would grapple in the arena of public opinion. Once the situation was set, Alex would be able to make his move.

He suddenly became dizzy. The bootleg meds were catching

up with him. He sat down and collected himself. The dreams of Africa were not as bad as they once had been. They had faded to rough, hazy images of pain, the jungle, and the sun.

He was aware that he was not operating at 100 percent. Sometimes he felt righteous in his quest. At other times he felt as though the whole thing was a bad dream from which he'd just awakened. The fabric of reality shifted constantly in his head, and only the contents of that black case and the items it had led him to in Baltimore, Philadelphia, and New York reminded him he was not completely insane.

Chinatown

Luther had found Alex. His street work wasn't nearly as neat as he wanted it to be. He'd been lied to, led down false paths, and generally fucked over in the last few days. But he had found what he needed to know about Alex's whereabouts, as well as the man called Nappy.

Nappy was a street alias. Hampton had discovered that Chokwe Muhammad was on the government's list of subversives. His father and mother were sixties radicals and known anti-American activists. It was also no surprise that Nappy was engaged in the drug trade and had somehow been recruited by Alex. Sharpie had been a valuable source of information in this regard.

Getting to Alex had also been complicated by the terror alert in Detroit. There were more cops than ever on the street, and under the Homeland Security Act they had greater powers to detain people. Luther did not fancy himself a political person. At best he was a cynic, but he always thought it sad that so many laws that sought to protect the people shredded parts of the Constitution to achieve their goal.

In the end Alex's race had betrayed him. There were not many white men frequenting the areas he traveled, and many people had "heard" about a white man who was handing out money and who was not to be trifled with. But no one had actually seen him. Even disfigured and desperate, Alex was still largely invisible.

Luther could barely restrain himself as he prepared to take Alex. A thudding rap tune by David Banner still echoed in his head as he slipped further into mission mode.

Hampton had reported back to Kilmer that they had found Alex. Luther wasn't sure whether that had been a good thing to do. He had his suspicions about this mission. E-1, like any covert government agency, was steeped in dangerous secrets and lies. Luther knew many stories about the agency and had been witness to what it would do to keep its secrets. And they'd all signed the *vita pactum*, which in a sense forfeited their lives to the agency.

Alex was speaking to Luther through this mission, and Luther had to know what he was saying before he completed the mission and neutralized Alex.

Alex was living in three places in Detroit. He had a far-east-side place, a protected house that he basically rented from a small-time drug dealer. He also had a motel room on the north side just south of Eight Mile Road. And he had the place Luther was now near, a tenement near Third and Porter in what had been home to Detroit's Asian community years earlier.

It figured that Alex would be here, Luther thought. His last crime had been committed not far away. And with the terror alert, Luther was sure that no one was working too hard to solve that crime.

The building was an old-style apartment house. Its name had

been Crest Manor, but all you could see was CR__T MA_OR on the stone lintel. There were only a few families living there, if you could call them families. The building was home to low-grade prostitutes, lower-grade dealers, and the normal people from the bottom rungs of life.

"There are many innocents in this building," said Hampton to Luther from his remote location.

"And Alex will not hesitate to endanger or kill them."

"Stay on him," said Hampton. "We can't afford to lose him again."

Luther didn't appreciate this comment, but he didn't say anything. He did plan to do just as Hampton suggested, though. An E-1 agent was not humane—he was purposeful. It was the fulfillment of his mission that was humane.

Luther attached a Janlow silencer to the end of the P99. It was a bit bulky, but the high-tech alloy would cut the noise to almost nothing.

Luther moved as little as possible. Alex was too smart to be taken completely off guard, so Luther's only hope would be to give him the least amount of time possible in which to react. If he remembered his capture-and-detainment lesson well, Alex would use lethal means to the fullest extent to protect himself. So when Luther made his move, Alex would try to destroy him and everything in his path.

Alex Deavers watched as Luther approached the building. Luther had found him much sooner than he'd anticipated. Then again, Luther had always been a superior student. Alex had left enough clues on the street for him, but Luther had obviously done more homework.

Alex wondered whether Luther had put any of his clues together yet. He had to know that something was amiss with this mission, that Kilmer and the big boys were involved in some shit that was extremely dangerous, even by E-1 standards.

This was it, Alex thought. All his planning had come to this moment. He would engage Luther here, and either Luther would join him in his quest or Alex would leave him dead in the streets of his hometown. He would not make the same mistake he'd made in London with Lisa.

Alex was suddenly possessed of that feeling that he was not quite sane. His head spun with the circular logic of it. He had to rely on the confidence in his heart that he was a functional human being who had done terrible things to achieve a noble goal. He had to be sane. That was the only way any of this made sense.

Alex composed himself and then looked out the window again. He saw his men waiting and the dark figure of Luther across the street. To an untrained eye, Luther could have been a bush, a shadow, or at most some bum lurking in the night. But Alex saw the deliberate movement of a man on a covert operation. It was his old student, all right, and Luther was doing everything by the book.

Alex would be careful not to injure Luther too badly. But he had to hurt him to make his point. You couldn't reason with an E-1 agent. He was a killer, and the only way to neutralize this attitude was to threaten him with the same type of death the agent hoped to inflict.

Nappy had brought two of his best men for this mission. The man who called himself Wolf had asked him to help defend against an assassin who had a beef with him. That had been days ago. They'd been camping out every night, waiting for the assassin to arrive.

Nappy knew most of the good street-level hitters in Detroit. The best of them were just sociopaths who were on their way to jail. This guy must be an out-of-towner, perhaps from Chicago or Cleveland. There was even a good one in Toledo he'd heard about a few years back.

Nappy had his two men, Menthol and Casey, posted in front and back of the house, respectively. Menthol got his name because of his chain-smoking. Casey was an import from Toronto. Both were smart and ruthless. Nappy was stationed a half block down the street, where he watched from the Buick. He had confidence in the two men, but just in case, Nappy had brought along his most trusted friend, a new Thunder Ranch .223 rifle, a nasty weapon made for gun nuts and NRA types. The Thunder Rifle would stop anything human. Nappy didn't like gunplay, but when he did shoot, he wanted to kill. In this city you didn't want to just wound a man.

The disfigured white man who had asked Nappy to call him simply Wolf was a great source of information, but Nappy was concerned that he didn't know what Mr. Wolf was planning. He told himself that it didn't matter, that after Wolf gave him more secret government information, he could take his business legit, create a new sense of political awareness for his people, get out of crime for financial support, and fulfill the dream of his father.

But his instincts told him something was wrong. Wolf had to be some kind of ex–government agent, CIA or NSA, to know the things he knew.

Mr. Wolf was holed up on the fifth floor of the place. Nappy didn't know how the hitter expected to get past his men and get to the top of that building without being killed. So why was Wolf worried about this hitter? Why not handle it himself? Nappy began to get more worried about it himself, and he was suddenly glad he'd brought the two men to engage the hitter first. If Wolf was afraid, then the hitter was bad news.

Nappy saw a man emerge from a house down the street—just appear, as if by some magic. Had he been there all along? Or was Nappy imagining it now? No, it was a man, a tall man, and he crept up the dark street a half block from Wolf's building. Then the tall shadow crossed the street and headed toward Menthol, who was guarding the front entrance and lighting up his tenth cigarette of the evening.

Nappy smiled. It would be a short night's work. Menthol and Casey would kill the man, dispose of the body. Wolf would thank Nappy and reward him with another subversive secret that would dazzle his readers. They would all be eating White Castles by ten o'clock.

Alex watched from his window as Luther circled toward the house. Luther would take the front man and then come straight to him on the fifth floor. Luther would wait and kill the rear guard, who would undoubtedly follow him in. Then he'd engage his target. Nappy would enter in the middle of the fight between Luther and himself. Luther would kill Nappy easily, but that would be his fatal mistake. While Luther killed Nappy, Alex would take him down. Then young Luther would get one chance to join him. If he answered wrong, Alex would have no choice but to end his life.

But he was forgetting something, Alex thought. He didn't know what, but a piece of this scenario was missing. These days there always seemed to be something slipping from his mind. Luther's approach was stealthy but still too orthodox for what he knew of the man. But Alex had left him no choice, really.

I am not insane, he kept telling himself. He knew what he was doing. He was right in mind and mission.

Alex watched as Luther stopped just in front of the guard. He was probably going to pretend to be some local guy looking for drugs. The guard would try to take him, and then the game would be on. Alex watched. His pulse quickened, and he felt his muscles tighten.

The man they called Menthol threw down his cigarette and said something to the man who was about ten yards or so in front of him. Menthol slowly began to step toward Luther.

Then Luther turned and ran.

Luther sprinted back up the street away from the building. Menthol immediately gave chase, leaving his post. Alex heard him yell something and assumed that the rear guard had been called to give chase as well.

And that was what was missing, Alex thought.

Luther's only chance to take him was by surprise, and Alex's only assumption had been that Luther had found this hiding place just days ago, but it seemed possible that Luther had been onto him for much longer.

That was not Luther down there on the street.

Alex was pulling out his gun when the back windows to his room exploded. Luther swung in on a harness and flew at him, landing on his old mentor and dislodging Alex's gun from his hand. Alex flung Luther off him. When Alex got to his feet, he ran to Luther and began an attack, inflicting fierce blows and trying to keep Luther from drawing his weapon.

Luther threw a punch that Alex easily avoided, but Luther switched direction of the same hand and landed a backhand to Alex's jaw.

Alex spun and raised a kick, which barely missed Luther's head. Luther struck again, this time also with a kick. Alex dodged and caught Luther in the ribs with a blow that made him back off.

Luther attacked again, and now he and Alex traded blows, each man doing damage. Alex struck at Luther's throat but missed. Luther wrapped his arm around Alex's outstretched wrist and pulled him forward onto his knees. Alex reeled backward from the blow.

Luther heard the footsteps coming before the door burst open. He drew back from Alex, and the last thing he saw was the sad expression that passed for a smile on his old mentor's face.

Luther ran to the door as Nappy and his men burst inside. Either the decoy outside had gotten away or they'd killed him. Menthol was the first through the door. Luther hit him across the throat, and the big man dropped his gun and tumbled forward.

Luther heard an explosion as Nappy fired the rifle. The shots missed him but tore a hole in the far wall.

In his peripheral vision, Luther saw Alex jump out the same window that Luther had come in through, landing on a fire escape.

Luther easily took the second man, Casey. He grabbed the man's outstretched gun hand, pointed the gun into the man's own thigh, and made him fire. Casey dropped to the floor, dropping the gun.

Luther got a look at the third man. He was tall and bald and carried a rifle. He fired again, ripping bullets wildly. Luther dove away, pulling his P99 and firing at the doorway. He heard the man back out of the room and run down the stairs.

Luther quickly walked to Casey and kicked him in the head, putting him out. Then he turned to Menthol, who was still on his knees, choking and gasping for air.

Luther put his gun to the side of the man's head. "Where can I find your boss?" he asked.

"Don't . . . know," he said feebly.

Luther stepped back from Menthol. As the man turned to look at him, Luther knocked him out cold.

Luther made a hasty retreat. It would be harder to find Alex now that he'd narrowly escaped. But Nappy was in the mission, too, and he was not as clever as the wolf.

Sweet Georgia Brown's

Luther was back on the street. Now he was looking for the man they called Nappy. It had been three days since he'd lost Alex in Chinatown. It was a tormenting failure that had nagged him each waking moment. He had outsmarted Alex, but to no avail. Nappy and his band of thugs had no idea what they were dealing with. Alex would backwash them all as soon as he got whatever he was after in Detroit.

It was painfully clear to Luther that Alex had changed the rules of covert urban operations. He was bringing others into the loop, forfeiting their lives, but that made it easier for him to operate against another agent. To catch him, Luther would have to do the same.

Hampton was out in another part of town trying to get info on Alex. He didn't know the city, and his complexion was probably going to hinder him, but he was giving it the old college try.

The city was still on high alert, and the Middle Eastern community had closed ranks against the local government. An Arab business had been torched, and the fire department had been accused of coming late to the blaze. The city was still crawling with cops, which made Luther nervous.

Tonight Luther was just off Gratiot Avenue east of downtown. This was part of the area controlled by Nappy.

It made Luther angry to think of the things Alex would promise a man who'd dedicated his life to working against his own government. And sure enough, Nappy's so-called newspaper, *The Radical*, had recently published several stories revealing secret government actions that only someone like Alex would know about.

Luther didn't care about Nappy's politics. Men who were anti-American were possessed of a special insanity. They were self-important fools who thought that the toppling of the established order would lead to greater power for themselves. They never saw that the end of government was the beginning of anarchy, and that was the end of civilization.

The Renaissance Center loomed in the background like a benevolent big brother to the shabbiness of the city below. Luther walked the neighborhood that lived in this shadow, with its dark streets and darker houses. The sidewalks were cracked, and some had gaping holes in them. The harshness of winter would rip up the concrete paving, and it always took the city the longest time to repair the poorest neighborhoods.

There was so much criminal activity here that it seemed legal. Luther had witnessed four drug buys and seen three men who were carrying weapons. It was just after nightfall, and the denizens of the city were out in force.

Today was Friday, and cars were rolling into downtown from all directions as people came into the city to gamble at the casinos and dine at the many fine restaurants. The night was warm, and

Luther felt just a hint of the terrible humidity that was to come in the summer.

He crossed Gratiot and moved closer to downtown, slowing as he spotted the man he was waiting for. Luther waved at a thin black man with dyed blond hair.

Luther had recruited Sharpie to impersonate him at Alex's hideout. Luther was happy when he found out Sharpie had escaped. He'd sent word that he was looking for him.

"Guess you surprised to see me, huh?" said Sharpie.

"Somewhat," said Luther. "How did you get away from them?"

"Too fast," said Sharpie. "That big dude was fat, and he was a smoker. You can't catch Sharpie when your ass is out of shape." He laughed and seemed pleased with himself.

Luther noticed that the man was nervous. Sharpie was one of those street people who tried to cover everything with a smile and an upbeat attitude. The other kind covered everything with anger. Luther didn't think much of it. After all, Sharpie had been chased by killers just days before.

"Did you get your white man?"

"I'm looking for someone else now," said Luther, ignoring the question. "Nappy."

"Shoot, you don't wanna be messin' with him, man," said Sharpie.

"Yes, I do."

"Your funeral," said Sharpie. "How much you payin' for this information?"

"Fifty," said Luther, and he said it like that was his final offer.

"Fifty?" said Sharpie, as if insulted. "Man, a nigga ain't gonna do nothing with your dangerous ass for that kinda money. Two hundred."

Luther just turned and walked away. Sharpie was no different from any other informant. He'd do it for nothing if he had to. You had to let him know you weren't about to negotiate with him at all. Foreign street people were easier to deal with. They usually had a price, and that was that. They accepted that they were scum. In America the lowlifes were so arrogant; they assumed they were actually doing business.

"Hold up," said Sharpie. "Damn, cain't even haggle with a nigga no mo'. Okay, I'll take a hundred."

"Fine. What you got?" asked Luther.

"These hos told me he been hangin' out in Greektown lately, playing the casinos, you know."

"You want me to pay you for secondhand information from prostitutes?"

"Yo, man, these ain't random, skanky hos. These bitches are high-class, tight and fine, just startin' out. Don't do a lot of drugs or nuthin'."

Luther almost laughed at the attempt to lend the women credibility. But in Sharpie's world it made sense. "Who is he hanging with in Greektown?" asked Luther, trying to hide his building excitement.

"Young girls, big dudes, you know how they roll."

Luther knew Greektown. It was a popular shopping and dining neighborhood. It was also home to a big casino. It was densely populated, and he worried about going there on a Friday night.

Luther gave Sharpie a hundred. "If it doesn't check out, I'll be looking for you," he said.

"No need. Remember, Sharpie can get ya."

Sharpie walked off quickly. Luther headed toward Greektown, covering his head with a Tigers cap and his eyes with a pair of sunglasses. The shades, which helped to disguise him, were also night-vision glasses that allowed him to see far more than he would have without them.

He tried to calm himself down. He'd botched the first acquisition attempt, and he was looking to redeem himself. But he had to keep a cool head. You become vulnerable to your enemy when you let emotion override logic.

Soon he was in Greektown and starting to look around. There were even more people than he'd expected, and now he wished that he'd worn some kind of real disguise. He moved quickly along the streets. Cop cars were everywhere, and Luther remembered that police headquarters was not far away, on Beaubien Street.

He struck out that night but returned on Saturday and then again on Sunday, still searching for Nappy.

Luther walked the streets, keeping his head down and eyes averted. When he passed one particular Greek restaurant, he stopped in his tracks. He saw a man dressed in black and wearing a hat. The man had his back turned and was standing at the end of a corner near the freeway. Quickening his pace, Luther headed toward him.

As Luther got closer, the man shifted on his feet and turned, revealing the face of Alex Deavers. Luther saw only a flash of it, and then Alex was off.

Luther went after him, dodging people and pulling his P99, then just as quickly putting it back. He'd been chasing Nappy but had found Alex. Luther had to get him before he did any harm to the many people around. He pursued Alex in a big circle and saw him dart into a restaurant. Luther followed, not noticing the sign that read SWEET GEORGIA BROWN'S.

Stepping into the restaurant, Luther scanned the place. He

saw a commotion at the back, and it seemed as though someone had just run out that way, knocking over a waiter.

Luther was about to go after him when he heard a familiar voice.

"Cricket?"

The word hit Luther like a shot to the head. A hand caught him by the elbow. Instinctively, Luther had begun to push the person away when he recognized the voice, and reality came crashing in on him. Alex had outsmarted him again. He'd had his own plan, and this was part of it. So was Sharpie, who had been turned like a double agent.

"Hello, Mama," Luther said.

"We thought maybe you were dead," said Theresa Green. She hugged her son. Roland, Luther's father, was sitting in the waiting area as well.

"Hey, son," said Roland. Luther hugged him.

"How you doin', big head?" asked his sister Mary. She was smiling and had a glittery bracelet on her wrist. Luther was reminded why they'd nicknamed her Mary Sunshine.

He was speechless. Alex had invoked Rule 35 as a warning to him. Luther's family was now part of this mission, whether he liked it or not. Alex had deliberately lured him here so that they would see him.

"What are you all doing here?" said Luther, removing his dark glasses.

"You invited us," said Theresa, who was crying now. "We got your letter a few days ago."

"You said to meet you here," said Roland. "I didn't know you even knew about this place. It's kinda new, after all."

"He don't look dead," said Mary. "Can we eat?"

"What you been doin', son?" asked Roland, a concerned look in his eyes. "Last we heard, you was overseas. You still in the military?"

"Are you married, Cricket?" asked Theresa.

"No, not married," said Luther. "I'm working for several military suppliers."

"You could visit more," said Theresa. "I might be dead, for all you knew."

"Can we eat?" asked Mary again.

Luther was dumbfounded. He had to get away from them, or something bad would happen. Was Alex threatening his family, or did he just want to slow Luther down? Against Luther's will the pleasing aromas of the restaurant's food invaded his body.

"Where's everybody else?" he asked warily. He was thinking about how many of his family were not yet within the rule. Micah, Ruth, and Thomas were not involved so far.

"Well, the rest knew about this but chose not to come," said his mother.

"It's okay," said Luther. "Uh, let's eat." Alex was gone, so now Luther had to make sure his family wasn't further compromised. If he ran out, they might try looking for him, and that would be bad. And something else. He missed them. He had to admit it; he missed seeing the familiar faces of his people.

"One more coming," said Mary.

"I thought you said the others were—"

Just then Vanessa Brown, Luther's high-school sweetheart, walked into the restaurant, looking almost exactly the way she had ten years before. She was tall and gorgeous. The glasses were gone, and she wore a pair of black pants that showed off every curve of her body, which was exquisite. She'd topped the pants with a crisp white shirt unbuttoned to the swell of her cleavage. He felt that tug in his gut, that pinching warmth that a boy feels the first time he realizes what girls were put here for.

She approached their table and smiled. Luther smiled back sheepishly. He didn't feel like a government assassin, a lethal weapon, and the key figure in a major investigation. He felt like a kid embarrassed when a teacher finds the love note he's tried to pass. Suddenly he was embarrassed at his hesitation. He didn't know what kind of look was on his face, but his mother was smiling so broadly that he could see every tooth in her mouth.

"Hey, Luther," said Vanessa.

"Hi, Vanessa." He moved closer to her but didn't feel himself do it, and from behind him he could feel his mother's urging smile and hopes for a quick wedding and grandbabies.

"She's 'Dr. Brown' now," said Theresa excitedly.

"Congratulations," said Luther. "I didn't know."

"No big deal," said Vanessa. "I'm a general practitioner. I guess I never was really decisive." She laughed. "So what do you do now?"

Instead of answering, he hugged her. She felt good, and now Luther was fighting more than memories. Vanessa was awakening desires that were best left undisturbed.

"We were just about to eat," said Luther.

"That's why I'm here," said Vanessa.

"Girl, how did you get into them pants?" asked Mary.

"Don't embarrass me," said Vanessa.

"You do look nice," said Luther.

"Yes, she does," said Theresa too quickly. "She's not married, you know, Cricket."

"Cricket," said Vanessa, smiling. "I remember that name."

Luther didn't want to remember it. He wanted to ask his mother to stop calling him that, but he knew she wouldn't. She needed it.

They ate, enjoying Sweet Georgia Brown's fabulously soulful cuisine. Luther dodged questions all night. His mother made him promise to come by her house.

Vanessa made small talk, but Luther could see she wanted to speak with him alone. He took her phone number but did not offer his own.

The meal was filled with dangerous questions about what Luther had been doing with his life. He handled them expertly, drawing from his memories of Theories of Manipulation class, a fancy name for the art of lying. His family now believed that he'd been traveling the globe for a military supplier.

They soon stopped questioning him about his life and moved on to the troubled lives of his siblings. It seemed the family was in chaos. His brother Micah was on drugs, and Ruth had two babies by two different men. Thomas had drifted from unemployment to worthlessness and was now flirting with crime.

Luther didn't know what the hell was going on. His family had never been a model of behavior, but before now they had always steered clear of most of the bad shit in the 'hood.

His parents had an answer for this. It was their theory that the family had fallen apart largely because of Luther's absence. They felt that the entire family had to get together and have a sort of inner intervention to solve the problem. Theresa even wanted to invite a minister, but Roland axed that idea.

Vanessa just stared into her plate, understanding that she was suddenly in the middle of an embarrassing family situation.

Luther was speechless. He could not allow this to happen.

Having them all in one place made it a perfect strike opportunity for Alex. He demurred on attending, but his parents vowed to have the meeting anyway. And now he remembered how determined they were when they set their minds to something. They were a formidable pair. They had built a life from nothing, but in the end the vagaries of inner-city life had stolen their power and reduced their children to statistics.

Luther sat frustrated by his secrets. He had no good choice here. Alex had plunged him into Rule 35, and it was just as awful as he had imagined. Family was the ultimate inconvenience to a government agent.

Dinner over, Luther said hasty good-byes to his family and Vanessa and then walked outside into the coolness of the night. He hated to leave them without protection, but he had no choice.

He had taken only a few steps when he realized that someone was following him. He quickened his pace and stepped behind a big SUV as if to cross the street, then waited at the rear of the vehicle. He could hear his pursuer approaching. Luther would have to disarm and neutralize him quickly, then go back to his family and make sure they were okay.

A shadow moved by the side of the SUV and stopped. To the pursuer, Luther had disappeared. Luther listened as the person hesitated, then took another step toward him. The shadow crept closer to the edge of the SUV, and Luther could wait no longer. He sprang from his hiding place and grabbed the man. His hand shot out to the pursuer's throat and squeezed tight. He was about to yank hard when he saw the lovely face of Vanessa.

"Vanessa?" said Luther.

"Luth—" she tried to say, but her wind was cut off. Luther let her go, and she coughed.

"Sorry," said Luther, feeling embarrassed.

Vanessa held up a hand to tell him either that it was okay or that she needed a moment to get her breath.

"Arch your back and breathe," said Luther.

Vanessa did, and soon she was better. Luther stood there on the dark street, letting go of all the instincts he'd almost used to kill his high-school sweetheart.

"I wanted to talk to you alone," said Vanessa.

"About what?" asked Luther in a voice that didn't sound like his own.

"It's gonna sound silly to you."

"Then just say it."

"Why did you disappear like that, leaving everyone you know behind?" The words tumbled out of her as if she'd been wanting to say them for a long time. You made us all feel like we weren't important, Luther."

Luther knew that he'd left behind a lot of damage when he joined E-1. He'd have to choose his answer carefully.

"I'm a government assassin," said Luther. "I travel the world and kill our enemies to protect truth, justice, and the American way."

"So you really aren't taking me seriously, are you?" said Vanessa, and for a second she looked like a pouting teenager.

"Vanessa, we can't go back," said Luther. "I made a choice a long time ago for whatever reason, and I've assumed a life that has taken me worlds away from the one I was headed for—the one we were destined for. Things are too different now for me to forget all that."

"I—" Vanessa started, then stopped herself and nodded. "I understand," she said. "I don't really know what I want from you,

Luther. I guess I'm just very curious, and I need some kind of personal closure."

"Closure is for people who have problems, Vanessa," said Luther. "We never had a problem. I was here in one life, and then I left for another. It's done."

"And me?" she asked.

"Part of the life I left," said Luther. And then, hearing the harshness in what he'd said, he added, "Regrettably."

Realizing that he'd brought the threat of harm and death to Vanessa and his family, Luther kissed her gently on the cheek. It was as much as he dared to do. He let the moment slip away and then turned his mind back to finding the wolf.

Luther walked off, leaving Vanessa behind and thinking about Alex somewhere in Detroit, laughing at him and planning his next move. He thought about Sharpie, who would probably be backwashed by Alex soon. But mostly he thought about the people whose lives were now potentially forfeit to his mission.

Turnabout

The Rough Riders tune pumped loudly in Luther's room the next morning. He was still in mission mode. He got up and called Hampton. Hampton came over, and they pulled themselves back into the mix.

"I searched the newspaper database for any story that might lead to the wolf," said Hampton.

"Anything?" asked Luther.

"The usual stuff about the growing anti-Arab sentiment and the terrorist alerts—and one other thing you might be interested in. The police database turned up a Eugene Sharpe, who died when he lost his footing on an overpass and fell into oncoming traffic on I-75 last night."

"Alex had Sharpie backwashed," said Luther.

"More than likely he had someone else do it," said Hampton. "Chucking a body onto a freeway is *not* E-1 style.

Luther wondered absently how many men Alex had working

for him, how much money he'd given them, and whether any of them knew that when he was done, he'd kill them.

"I have a theory," said Hampton. "Would you like to hear it?"

"Do I have a choice?" asked Luther.

"No. I think the wolf is behind the heightened terror alert."

"Why?" asked Luther.

"Unknown at this time, but the growing number of attacks on the Arab community has the stink of black ops."

"Yes," said Luther. "They seem planned, measured. The question is . . ."

"Why?" Hampton finished. "I don't know, as I said, but I have another theory that I'm sure you'll agree with. Whatever the reason is, you're integral to it."

"Alex knows about my family," said Luther. "And in Detroit there are many ways for him or a man like Nappy to reach out and cause harm to them in order to draw me out. Rule 35 isn't mandatory; it's designed to give an operative an advantage as a last resort."

Luther had sent his family and Vanessa back to their lives, oblivious to any danger they might be facing. He was sure that Alex wasn't threatening them directly. It was just a warning—for now.

Luther's Ion sounded. He answered it on the first ring.

"Wolf here," said the strained voice of his old mentor.

For an instant Luther was thrown into a state of shock. Alex was clever indeed.

"How did you get this number?" he asked as he mouthed Alex's name to Hampton.

"No way," said Hampton. He connected Luther's Ion to his computer and then patched it in to E-1.

"I didn't teach you *all* my tricks," said Deavers. "It took time, but I finally got the right codes."

"They'll just change them tomorrow," said Luther.

"It won't matter," said Deavers. "I'll only need the number this one time. So did you kill your TWA yet?"

"No. Is that why you called?"

"He'll turn on you in the end, Luther. And tell him that by the time he finds out how I got into the system, this call will be over."

"You know I won't do that," said Luther.

"You could shoot him now while he's on the computer."

"Your sense of humor has grown very dark, my friend," said Luther.

"If you can't laugh at yourself, you should die," said Alex.

"You're not well," said Luther. "You were almost killed. Can you be sure of what you're doing?"

"Maybe not," said Alex with a trace of a sigh. "Will you blindly follow orders, or will you question the home office?"

"I have my mission, and I will complete it," said Luther defiantly.

"Even at the expense of your loved ones?" Alex sounded superior, and at this moment he was.

"Just tell me what you're up to." Luther was stalling, trying to think of a way to get more information out of him.

"You needed to be trained as an agent—or in this case *re-trained*—by me. I wanted to open your mind to the possibility that your agency isn't what it seems. Did Kilmer let you work on that heating unit, or did he order you to leave, find me, and allow people to die?"

"You coordinated the whole thing?" Now Luther wasn't

stalling. He was impressed. "You're sick, Alex, and you're having paranoid delusions."

"If that's true, then we're both dead, my friend. I'll be in touch."

The line went dead. Hampton disconnected the Ion and saved the digital file, for what it was worth.

"He doesn't sound crazy," said Luther.

"Then he'll kill your family," said Hampton.

"If Alex employs Rule 35 against me, so be it."

"You're willing to sacrifice your family that easily?"

"It's my job. I knew the risks when he led me here."

"If it were my family, I'd do anything I could to save them," said Hampton.

"You are the most by-the-damned-book agent I know," said Luther. "All of a sudden you have a heart?"

"We can stop the wolf," said Hampton, not responding directly to Luther's challenge. "He's been smart, but his weakness is that he has employed civilian subagents. We've been unable to get to him, but maybe we can use his man Nappy against him."

Suddenly Luther smiled broadly. "Yes, we can. And since he's a part of Alex's team, perhaps Rule 35 can help us now."

Jewel was walking quickly away from school. She'd cut her last two classes, hidden in the girls' room, and sneaked out through the cafeteria, which was safe passage because the old men and women who worked there never told on you. She figured that they were bitter about their jobs and could care less if some kid wasn't getting the supreme knowledge afforded by the Detroit public schools.

She rounded a corner and saw a car coming her way. It was a tricked-out Lincoln Navigator, and she ran behind some bushes to hide from it. It could be one of her uncle's soldiers, and she couldn't let them see her. If Uncle Chokwe found out that she was cutting class, he'd be pissed, and the first thing he would do is stop giving her money. The second thing . . . well, she didn't want to think about it.

Jewel loved her uncle Chokwe, but he was too old-fashioned. All he talked about was boys and having sex and how it would ruin her life. At first she thought he was right. The boys were silly and hormonal. Many of them screwed her friends and then told everybody about it, something that terrified her. She was sure that she'd be a virgin for the rest of her life.

And then she met Veshawn. He had been a senior at her school before she ever got there. He was a popular guy and a star on the basketball team. Veshawn was tall and muscular and had an easy smile like that other basketball player, Chris Webber.

Veshawn was a dealer, but he sold only weed. She knew that her uncle Chokwe was into the drug trade, or at least that was what Rita always said. Jewel wondered at first whether Veshawn worked for her uncle, but he didn't. Veshawn was a rarity in the city: an independent.

The Navigator passed, and Jewel moved on, hooking a turn at a corner and then moving swiftly up the street. She saw Veshawn's car, a Mercedes, parked in the driveway of a modest little house, and she went to the side door and knocked hard.

Veshawn came to the door wearing nothing but a smile. His penis was erect, and Jewel smiled at the sight of it.

"What you want?" he asked casually.

"I'm lookin' at it," said Jewel. "Now, let me in before somebody sees me."

Jewel had been having sex with Veshawn for more than a year. He had slowly seduced her with smooth talk, soft kisses, and lots of presents.

Jewel told Veshawn about her uncle, and for a while Veshawn was afraid to see her. He knew about the man called Nappy, and he understood that screwing Nappy's only niece would mean his death if Nappy found out.

But Jewel persisted with him. She liked his deep, silky voice, his big hands, and the way he kissed her, sucking at her tongue and giggling like a schoolboy. He was amazed by her body and looked at her like a hungry animal. This made her feel powerful and beautiful, something that was a treasure in the hardness of her life.

"I love you," said Jewel as they made love. Veshawn grunted something like "Me, too," and descended on her breasts. Jewel exploded with feeling and sensation. Slowly the world around her melted away, and she let her passion consume her. As she was lifted by her desire and then her fulfillment, she kept telling herself that this could not possibly be wrong.

Two hours later Jewel emerged from the house and got into a car with Veshawn. He drove her to a spot several blocks from her house, then let her out. She again told him that she loved him, then kissed him good-bye.

Jewel walked the last few blocks to her house, already practicing her post-sex demeanor. It was a routine she was used to. As Jewel got to her house and was about to walk up the steps, she heard a noise behind her. She never saw the man who had followed her from Veshawn's house. Her first thought was that it was her uncle or one of his men. But she didn't recognize the face of the man who stood behind her, then moved closer, stopping her from entering the house.

The Patriot

Nappy sat quietly as his mother raged at him in the little house. He felt like a kid again as she rolled through her hurt and pain at the disappearance of her only granddaughter.

Rita stood by with her fat arms folded across her fatter chest, shooting lasers at Nappy. This was a victorious moment for Rita. Jewel was gone, maybe dead, and Tawanna blamed Nappy for it.

Jewel had been missing since the end of the school day, and no one knew where she was. Jewel was a good student, and it was unlike her to miss any classes. Nappy feared the worst—that his protection had faltered and some neighborhood thugs had gotten to her for whatever stupid-ass reason they were using this week.

The thought of what those kinds of men would do to her made him sick to his stomach and angry enough to kill.

"We have to call the police," said Tawanna. She was almost shaking with hurt and fear.

"No," said Nappy. "No cops. I told you I'll find her." He had all his forces on the street looking for her. So far the only thing they'd learned was that she had cut her last two classes.

"This is your fault," said Tawanna. "You and your bullshit have finally got her caught up in something terrible."

"*My* fault?" said Nappy incredulously. "You're the one who won't move out of this place. I offered—"

"I told you I don't want your money!" Tawanna screamed. "By the grace of God, I've kept you in my heart, but that's where I drew my line."

"I said I was going to find her, and I will!" yelled Nappy. "These are my streets, and if she's out there, I'll get to her!"

"Who the fuck are you? Batman?" sneered Rita.

"Shut up, you fat bitch!" said Nappy. "You're not in this family. Go clean up something and stay the fuck out of grown folks' business."

Nappy got up and had it in his head to just kick Rita's ass. That would make him feel better, he thought. He had control over that, and he'd do it—bash her fat little head in until she stopped breathing. As he took a step toward her, he felt his mother grab his arm.

"What are you doing, boy? Leave her alone and find my grand-baby," ordered Tawanna.

Nappy blinked hard, pulling himself from the murderous feeling in his head. He stopped moving toward Rita and drew his mother to him. Nappy kissed Tawanna and walked out the door.

He got into the Buick and drove off, at the same time and dialing a number on his cell phone.

"Talk to me," he demanded.

"We got something," said a young man on the line. "But you ain't gon' like it."

"Just tell it, muthafucka," said Nappy.

"Your niece got a boyfriend, some dude named Veshawn. One of his boys told us. He's been hittin' it regular, from what we heard."

Cursing, Nappy turned the car around and headed toward the address he was given. He was soon at the Nevada address. He saw his crew's car parked outside but no sign of the men themselves. They must be inside. He cursed again, loudly. They'd engaged the boyfriend and had probably gotten into a fight. He prayed that Jewel was there but hoped she hadn't witnessed any violence. Nappy swore to himself that if they had done anything to Veshawn, he'd kill them all.

Nappy entered the house. Just inside the front door, he stopped cold in his tracks. His two men were lying in a heap on the floor, bound together. Standing next to them was the man Wolf had sent them to capture. Beside him was a scared young man tied to a chair. That had to be Veshawn. Before Nappy could react, Luther closed the gap between them.

"Give me your gun," said Luther.

Nappy saw that Luther was not armed. He instantly went to reach for his gun. As soon as he did, he felt something being jammed into the small of his back.

"Don't be foolish," said Hampton from behind him.

Nappy froze. Luther moved closer and took Nappy's gun from him.

Hampton pushed Nappy farther into the room and then stepped around in front of him. He kept the Baby Eagle trained on Nappy.

"Where is she?" Nappy asked.

"Safe, if you cooperate," said Luther.

"I'm gonna kill you," Nappy said, pointing a finger at Veshawn. Veshawn cringed as if he'd been struck. Nappy took a step toward the cowering man, but Hampton waved him back with his gun.

"Now, now, fellas, let's not fight," said Luther. He took a step away from Nappy and turned as if to leave. Then he spun on his heel, raised a foot, and kicked Nappy on the chin, dropping him.

Hampton went to Veshawn and untied him.

"If I were you, I'd get as far from Detroit as I could," said Hampton. "And for the record, you should be ashamed of yourself."

They secured Nappy and took him out of the house, leaving his men behind. In the car they administered a tranquilizer so that he would not come to. Then they drove away.

"Okay," said Hampton. "Now what?"

"I get him to talk," said Luther.

"And if he doesn't?"

"We kill the girl." Luther waited a beat and then laughed. "Just kidding."

"Not funny," said Hampton. "You want me to help out?"

"No. I don't want him to know who you are. I might need you later."

"But if you get the info on the wolf, you'll call me in."

"Of course."

Luther dropped Hampton off at their safe house and then took Nappy to the one place that he knew Alex would never think to look for him. Alex's Chinatown address had been abandoned, and local thieves had pretty much cleaned the place out. It would be a good place to hide.

Once he was settled in, Luther called his family just to make sure they were all right. His mother answered the phone, sounding cheerful. His siblings had agreed to have the family meeting, and she was delighted.

"I don't know when I can do it," said Luther. "I have lots of loose ends here in Detroit."

"Well, we can't keep this out there too long," said Theresa.

"I know, Mama, but business first."

He heard Ruth's voice in the background.

"I got a package?" said Theresa. Then to Luther she said, "I'm sorry. This girl is about to worry me to death about some pretty box. Listen, your father wants to talk to you for a minute."

"I can't," said Luther. "Tell Daddy I'll call him back later. I promise."

He hurried her off the phone without giving her a number where she could call him. Luther knew he was really upsetting her, but it was for the best. He wanted so much to tell her she might be in danger, but he had to accept what his profession meant for him and his loved ones. They were in this now, and he prayed that Alex was not nearly as far gone as Luther suspected.

When Nappy came to, he found himself seated in a broken old chair, one of the few pieces of furniture that had been left behind.

"That stuff I gave you is good, huh?" said Luther. He hadn't tied Nappy up. If this was going to work, he had to make Nappy feel that Luther was the lesser of the two evils facing him. Luther had to remember that this civilian was a criminal and in a way almost an agent himself.

"Where's my niece?" asked Nappy groggily. He got to his feet, then thought better of it and sat back down.

"Where's my friend?" asked Luther.

"Wolf?"

"Yes," said Luther, quickly realizing what the name meant. This was more of Alex's sick humor.

"I don't know. He's a sneaky muthafucka, just like you."

"You're going to bring him to me—tonight. However it is you contact him, do it. The rest is mine, and then your niece will be back home safe and sound. That's the deal. No negotiating."

"I'm not stupid," said Nappy. "I know you and your friend Wolf are government agents. Black ops and all that shit. Only he got smart and turned. And look at you, a black man, the good boy holding down the fort for your master."

"You got it wrong," said Luther. "I'm a patriot."

Nappy laughed at him, a husky laugh that shook his body. "A black patriot. Do you know how stupid that sounds?"

"Patriotism is a principle that teaches that nothing is greater than the ideal of America. Now, my country wants you to tell me what I want to know—or, in the name of patriotism, I will kill you."

"I don't turn on my friends. I won't give you Mr. Wolf."

"What about your niece?"

Without the slightest change in expression, Nappy said, "Some things you just have to take."

Luther watched Nappy carefully as he said these words. His training told him that Nappy was lying, trying to see how much leverage he could muster. Nappy had spoken defiantly, but as he had, he'd dropped his eyes from Luther. That was a "tell," a sign he didn't believe his own action.

Luther didn't respond. If he talked, Nappy would know he was calling his bluff, and the game could go on forever. Luther had to make Nappy think he was going to kill him right then and be done with it. And it would follow that his niece would die as well. Luther believed that Nappy had accepted his own death, but he didn't believe he'd accepted that his young niece would die.

Luther looked Nappy in the eyes, thought about the terrible things Nappy did on the streets to people, to children, then pulled his P99 and raised it as quickly as he could in a fluid motion.

"Wait!" said Nappy. "Hold up, dammit!"

"Make it good," said Luther from behind the big gun.

Nappy took in a sharp breath, then let it out. "I have to call him from three different places within a time period, and then he meets me."

"I'll go with you," said Luther.

"How do I know you'll return my niece when I'm done?" asked Nappy.

"Easy," said Luther, lowering the gun. "I'm the good guy."

Nappy drove Luther's Ford as they went to the three locations and made calls. They had to be careful, as the streets were crawling with local police and unmarked cars that Luther could tell were standard FBI issue. He even saw what he believed was a CIA utility van. The terrorism alert had turned the city into a police state, he thought. The commotion over terrorism was a perfect diversion for an agent on a mission.

It was safer for Luther to let Nappy drive, as that way Luther's hands would be free to counter anything that might happen. Each location was near a party store in east, west, and southwest Detroit. At one phone a kid who had to be a drug dealer waited for a call. As soon as he saw Nappy, he ran off. Luther thought about the kind of fear this man instilled in the criminal populace. He was riding with the devil, he told himself. No matter, Luther thought. Tonight he, not Nappy, was the most dangerous man in Detroit.

Nappy finished the last call and then came back to Luther in the Ford.

"Now I meet him over by Palmer Park," said Nappy.

"And how do you know that?" asked Luther.

"Because last time I met him near John R Street and the time before that over by Hamtramck. These are the three places we meet. We rotate between them."

Standard drop procedure, thought Luther. Still, there was something about the locations that made him nervous, something in his training about rendezvous points and structures. He struggled to recall it.

Luther drove from the last location to Palmer Park, which was near the north end of the city close to Eight Mile.

"Now, where's my niece?" asked Nappy.

"When I see Wolf." Luther almost said Alex's real name.

"If she's been hurt, there's no place you'll be able to hide from me."

"I'll try not to worry about that." Luther could not suppress his smile.

"How many men have you killed?" asked Nappy.

"How many children have you poisoned?" Luther retorted.

"Don't give me that false morality."

"We all know who we are. Nothing that happens tonight will change that."

Luther heard himself speak these words, but he wondered whether they were true. Would his apprehension of Alex change him? If he failed, would his old mentor murder him and go on with whatever his personal mission was here in Detroit?

Nappy pulled the Ford onto a street next to Palmer Park. They got out, and Nappy led him across the street and into the park. It was dark out, and Luther walked several steps behind Nappy. Nappy moved toward a grove of trees. The light from the nearby street faded even more, and darkness rapidly enveloped them. Luther slowed his pace, and soon Nappy was well out in front.

Nappy stopped by a large twisted tree. He waited a moment, and when he turned, Luther was gone.

"What the . . . ? What kinda goddamned game you playin' now, nig—"

Nappy had not finished his thought when he was struck in the chest by something. He stumbled backward from the blow, and then he saw him. Alex stood in front of him. He pulled a knife and swung it so quickly that Nappy did not have time to draw another breath.

Luther grabbed Alex's long, dark coat and pulled him backward as he struck with the knife. This gave Nappy time to thrust up his arms. Nappy caught the edge of the knife on the meaty part of his left forearm. He felt the warm rush of blood and yelled in pain.

Alex turned and met Luther's foot. The blow caused Alex to drop the knife.

Nappy saw his chance and ran off into the night, not looking back and not caring who would win the fight.

Luther remembered why the three locations had unnerved him so. A structured rendezvous always invited surveillance. Alex had a transmitter at each one of the stations, which meant that he would be waiting at the drop point.

Alex assumed a fighting position, and Luther threw a punch that he easily blocked. The two men squared off. Luther had his gun, but he was determined not to kill his old mentor.

"I suppose your answer to joining me is no, then?" asked Alex.

Luther ran at him and threw a series of punches and kicks. Alex caught most of them, but the last punch sent him reeling backward. He fell to the ground.

"If you stop now, I'll spare your family," said Alex, getting up.

Luther said nothing, but he was sure Alex was not bluffing. Luther had already made his peace with Rule 35. His family was in some danger this night—they were Alex's backup plan. And in that same moment, he had a notion of exactly what that plan was.

"*I got a package?*" He heard his mother's voice. A bomb. The bastard had sent his mother a bomb.

Alex smiled in the darkness, that crazy thing that passed for a smile.

"The gravity of my being here has not occurred to you," said Alex. "Either you give in to me or they die."

Luther was enraged, but he quelled his anger. Alex wanted him to be angry. Strong emotion would throw him off. Luther swiftly assessed the situation. If there was a bomb, he'd have to get Alex quickly. If there wasn't, then it didn't matter. In either case he had to act in a measured fashion. He would not blow getting the wolf just to save his family. It sounded bad, but that was his job.

Luther blocked a kick and caught Alex around the neck. Alex drove his heel into Luther's foot, and Luther yelled. He threw Alex aside and jammed an elbow into his ribs. Alex countered with a blow to Luther's jaw, dropping him. Alex was about to administer a lethal blow when Luther heard a popping sound and saw Alex's head bob forward. He fell on his face, revealing Hampton standing behind him.

"Where the hell were you?" asked Luther.

"Shit, it's dark out here," said Hampton. "You're lucky I didn't hit *you*."

"What did you hit him with?" asked Luther, getting up.

"The newest knockout drug. It's a neural-impact compound that literally shuts down portions of the brain."

"Good," said Luther. They couldn't have Alex waking up in the middle of transport.

"Okay," said Hampton. "You do what you have to do to him. I don't want to see it." Hampton gave Luther a solemn look. He did not like the idea of executing an unconscious man. Shooting or killing someone in the heat of battle was one thing, but now that they had Deavers safe and sound, taking him out seemed barbaric.

"I'm not going to kill him," said Luther. "Not until I talk to him."

"What!?" Hampton almost yelled. "You said we'd take him first, but I assumed that you meant to eliminate him soon after."

"Marcellus," said Luther. He never called Hampton by his first name, and the use of it now made him pay close attention. "You cannot deny that something is wrong with this mission. Just trust me a little while longer. Meet me back at the base. I'll explain later."

Hampton walked off muttering. He was a creature of duty, and the rules meant everything to him. Luther hoped that Alex hadn't been right about the dangers Hampton might present.

Luther carried his prize away. There was no sign of Nappy, although Luther did see specks of blood by light of the street-lamp, which meant that Nappy had come back across this path. Although there was no one in sight, Luther was sure some jogger or dog walker had spotted or heard the fight and would call the police.

Luther thought about what Alex had said about the bomb as he drove off onto Woodward Avenue, his mission successfully completed. But there was no cause for celebration. Luther was miles away from his family and would never get to them in time. He doubted that his old mentor had left much of a margin for error. They were both trained killers, after all, and this was the deadliest of games.

Luther Green quietly accepted the fate of his occupation and the awful consequence that his family would probably be dead by the end of the night.

EXECUTIONER'S GAME

When an operative is certain that his agency or the governing body controlling it has been corrupted, the operative shall take all measures necessary to eradicate the corrupting influence and restore justice to all concerns.

—E-1 Operations Mission Manual, Rule 225

The Pretty Box

Alex was safe in the cab of Luther's Ford and sleeping peacefully. Luther quickly took out his cell phone and called his mother. He expected to hear a busy signal, a continuous ring, or, worse, nothing at all—all signs that the house had been blown to hell—but instead he got a ring and the line was picked up. He heard loud chatter in the background.

"Hello," said Luther.

"Luther?" said his mother.

"Yes," he said, trying not to betray the relief he felt. They were all still alive—for now. "Hey, who's there with you?"

"Just me and your father," she said.

He wanted to start asking her about what kind of package had arrived, but he didn't have time. His family had to get out of that house immediately. If he told her about the bomb, there would be too much explaining to do, and when it got out to the press, he'd be pulled from the mission.

"Mama," said Luther as calmly as he could. "I need to see

you and Daddy right now. Meet me at that restaurant we were at."

"Sweet Georgia's?"

"Yes."

"But it's Saturday night," said Theresa. "It's probably crowded. Why don't you just come over—"

"No time," Luther cut her off. "Just come." He tried to block out images of his family blown apart, but he couldn't. He saw his mother dismembered, lying in the street amid the still-burning debris of her beloved kitchen. And he saw his father split into tiny, bloody bits all over the street.

"Okay."

"Mama," said Luther, "that package you received. Where is it?" He still struggled to stay measured.

"It's in the living room," she said. "Don't know what's in it or who sent it. I tried to open the darn thing, but it has no way to open that I can see."

Alex must have used a security container so that the bomb would go off when he wanted it to.

"Okay," said Luther, "I might as well tell you. I sent that box. It's a surprise. Just leave it at home, and I'll open it for you later."

"Okay," said Theresa. "Come on," she called. "Let's go, Roland."

Luther hung up and drove as quickly as he could to his mother's house. He fought the images of fire trucks and police crowded around the charred remains of the house. He was fighting with himself about all of this. He wasn't supposed to care. Rule 35 didn't call for your family to be killed, but it was a possibility that any agent had to deal with. However, this mission was like no other he'd ever been on, and the rules, as sacred as they were, didn't seem to apply anymore. He'd already broken them anyway by not killing Alex, he thought.

When he got to his mother's house, it was still standing. The family car was gone, and the house looked deserted.

For a second he thought that maybe the bomb was a fake like the one in New York, but it was unlikely that Alex would bluff twice.

Luther still had Alex safely tucked in the cab of the Ford. He would find the device and disarm it. Alex couldn't have rigged anything too elaborate—he hoped.

He found the pretty box in a hallway closet. Luther took the box and left his mother's house as fast as he could. On the way out, he jostled a few things and left a window open. His family would think they'd been burglarized.

Luther took the box into his Ford and pulled away. He didn't know how much time he had before it went off. He drove about a mile to a deserted area and then looked at the box. Sure enough, it was in a security case, which Luther easily opened by pressing a sequence of hidden latches.

Inside, Luther found a BEP 12 that was wired and hot. BEP stood for Blake Explosive Pack, a powerful and deadly device. The bomb had a timer with several hours still left on it. If Luther hadn't found it, it would have detonated late that night.

Luther disarmed it and headed back to the safe house. He was relieved, but unsettled at how close he'd come to losing his parents.

Lynch

Nappy's freshly bandaged arm throbbed dully as he pulled up to his mother's house. The girl who had done it for him was a nurse at one of the local hospitals, and for a fee she'd doctored him and some of his men many times in the past. Thank God he hadn't been hurt worse, he thought.

He was sure he'd get an earful for not finding Jewel, but he wanted to let his mother know that he was still on the case.

He didn't know how he was going to deal with the murderous Wolf and his even deadlier friend. Maybe, if he was lucky, they'd killed each other. That was unlikely, he thought, and in the next instant he was rooting for Wolf's friend. At least *he* hadn't tried to kill Nappy.

He knocked only once on the door before it opened and Rita stood there, looking evil and pissed off.

"It's him," she said over her shoulder.

Rita stepped back and walked into the house. Nappy followed. In the living room, he found his mother sitting next to a still-frightened Jewel. Upon seeing her uncle, Jewel flew from the sofa and ran to him.

Nappy was so relieved he ignored the pain that shot into his arm when his niece embraced him. "Where were you?" he demanded.

"This man grabbed me, a white man," said Jewel. "He took me to a room in the back of the mall and locked me in. He took my cell phone."

"Who did he say he was?" asked Nappy.

"DEA," said Jewel. "He said he was going to raid our house, and he didn't want anyone to get hurt. He had a badge and everything. I was there for a long time, and finally mall security let me out. They thought I was crazy."

"We found your boyfriend," said Nappy, looking angrily at her.

"She's my responsibility," said Tawanna, standing up next to Jewel.

"Mama," said Nappy, "she's having sex with a grown man."

"I know," said Tawanna.

Nappy was silent for a moment. He looked into his mother's eyes, then to Jewel, and he saw it, the solidarity of the women against him. His mother had known and had done nothing.

"You knew?" he said incredulously.

"There are things a lot worse in this world than a young girl having a boyfriend."

"Ain't this a bitch?" said Nappy, shaking his head in disbelief. "You call this being a mother?"

"I'm not going to listen to *you* insult me in *my* house, boy. Get out, and don't come back as long as you're dealing in filth. Go."

"I'm not leaving here until we settle this thing with Jewel," said Nappy. "I—"

Just then he heard the familiar sound of a gun cocking behind him. He looked over his shoulder and saw Rita holding a .45 on him, aimed at his chest.

"The woman said get out," said Rita. "Which one of those words don't you understand?"

Nappy turned completely toward Rita and took a half step. He was shaking with anger. His fists tightened, and this time nothing would stop him from tearing the old woman apart one limb at a time.

"Go on," she said, raising the gun to his face. "Give me the reason."

Nappy stopped and turned back to his mother, but she was already pulling Jewel away from her uncle. Nappy again looked at Rita and the big gun.

"That's your ass, old bitch," Nappy almost snarled at her.

"Maybe," said Rita. "But right now you're *my* bitch."

Nappy tried to smile, to hide the fact that he had just been punked by an old woman. He went to the door and walked out.

Nappy got into his car, mumbling curses. He had a man just two streets over. He was going to get a gun and come back and settle with Rita tonight. He wasn't going to hurt her, he told himself. He would just let her know who the man was. He started his car and drove off.

When he stopped at a light, a dark SUV pulled up next to his car. He saw only a glimpse of the face in the passenger seat, but he recognized the grim visage of one of his rival street dealers, a man called Lynch.

Nappy thought about all the time he'd spent working with Wolf, all the time he'd tried to make his newspaper legit. He thought about the information provided by Wolf and how delighted it had made Nappy to know that he'd been right all these years about the government and how that knowledge seemed to lift him up and away from the source of his funding, the street.

He thought how those days spent away from the street were like years in the drug world, which moved fast. He could see the breakdown of his troops as they sensed he was slipping and felt the confidence a man like Lynch engendered in the feeble young minds of inner-city drug dealers who were all looking for lost fathers. He had abandoned them in their quest for manhood and their brief share of the American dream, the same dream he was working hard, through his newspaper, to reveal as a fraud. Irony, he thought, was a muthafucka.

Nappy saw the barrel of a gun move in front of the evilly smiling man and then the bright light of the muzzle flash as it fired point-blank into his face.

Deuce and a Quarter

Luther took Alex to a new location, a house in the city of Ferndale that he had arranged for through the agency in anticipation of capturing the wolf. It was a small place that sat back from the street. The front yard was wide and long and away from every other house on the block, perfect for what he had in mind.

Luther had called the restaurant and left word for his family that he'd been detained on business. His mother would be angry, but angry was better than dead.

"What took you so long?" asked Hampton.

"I had to steal a bomb from my mother's house," said Luther.

"What!?" said Hampton. "Where is it?"

"In the Ford. Alex sent it to my family."

"You brought it back here?" Hampton looked alarmed.

"It's disabled. Let's get him secure first," said Luther.

"It wasn't our mission to secure him, Luther," said Hampton.

"Let's not argue now," said Luther. "Help me."

Luther and Hampton put Alex into a patio chair which

Hampton had modified with secure devices. The chair was made of thick, heavy wrought iron. They chained Alex's arms and legs and then checked him for weapons. Alex had another smaller Japanese dagger, a .9mm gun, and three steel flying stars. Luther placed these items far away from the still-unconscious man.

Then he took out his Ion and got onto the E-1 secure network. Kilmer answered his private line on the first ring.

"Hello, sir," said Luther. He put the director on the speaker so both he and Hampton could hear.

"I would hope this is good news," said Kilmer.

"It is, sir," said Luther. "My mission is complete."

"Good," said Kilmer, who couldn't hide the excitement in his voice. "So what does the postmission situation look like?"

"There's cleanup to do, but for the most part we're fine," said Hampton.

"We're going to need to know everything Alex did," said Kilmer. "I want you to lead a team and find everything Alex had possession of. When you find it, destroy it immediately."

"Sir," said Hampton, "that's not quite the correct procedure."

"It's what I want to happen," said Kilmer. "Just do it."

"What are we looking for?" asked Luther. He remembered Kilmer's statement that Alex was *"in possession of that information, too."* Now he wanted to know what that meant. "Sir, am I looking for something specific?"

"No," said Kilmer quickly. "It will be a general search, just to make sure our priorities are secure. Tell me, how did you dispose of him?"

"I haven't," said Luther. Kilmer had obviously assumed that Alex was dead. "I have him here with us, alive."

There was silence on the line for a few seconds. Only the distant crackle of the connection. Finally Kilmer said, "I am disappointed."

"Sir," said Luther, "Alex was up to something here in Detroit, and I think we're close to knowing what it was."

"It's not your job to question, Luther. You will complete your mission right now. Neutralize Alex Deavers."

Luther's hand went absently to his P99. The innate instinct of the killer was already working out the execution. Kilmer was right. The agency had been created with the mandate of doing just what Kilmer had suggested, being the protector without judgment, reason, or emotion—killing without question.

Luther's sense of duty and honor rose within him, and his grip tightened on the gun. And then he thought of Rule 35, a rule that called for the potential killing of loved ones in favor of the very feeling of duty that swelled inside him. He'd walked away from his entire life in service of his country, yet on this mission he had gone to great lengths to preserve people from that life, and he had done so even though the strict letter of the law forbade it.

Luther's grip on the gun loosened, and from somewhere in the conditioned and closed-off regions of his heart, he came to the conclusion that his actions of late had made him a bad agent but perhaps a better man.

"No," said Luther.

Another deadly silence rose, and Luther looked at the little phone as if it were death itself.

"Then you have made your choice," said Kilmer. "Agent Hampton, relieve Agent Green."

Luther turned to see Hampton with his sidearm raised at Luther's head. He had put a silencer on the weapon, and it was cocked and ready to fire.

"Sorry, Luther, but I tried to tell you," said Hampton. "You can't countermand an order within a mission without—"

"Put that gun away," said Luther.

"Sir, what are my orders?" Hampton asked Kilmer.

"Complete the mission. Neutralize Deavers *and* Green."

Hampton fired. Luther reeled backward and landed faceup on the floor. Hampton walked over to him and fired another shot. Then he went to the still-unconscious Alex and fired twice more. He then returned to the phone.

"It's done, sir," he said, breathing heavily.

"Good," said Kilmer. "The cleanup team is coming soon. Dispose of the bodies. Then find where Deavers hid his materials and destroy them."

"Yes, sir," said Hampton. "Sir, I've been wanting to move up to regular fieldwork. I'd like to talk about that with you when I return."

"I can assure you a field assignment," said Kilmer. "It took great character to do what you just did. See me first thing."

"Yes, sir."

The line went dead.

Hampton sat down hard in a chair, saddened by what he'd just done. All his glory as an agent had ended in this moment.

"You didn't have a choice," said Luther. He'd fallen as loudly as he could to make it sound good for Kilmer. "He's not dealing honestly with us."

"He's the director," said Hampton. "He doesn't have to."

"Destroy evidence and kill the one witness who can clear all this up? He has no right to do that. No one has. Not to mention that situation in New York. We could've let hundreds of innocent citizens die for whatever he's hiding."

"We're both disgraced agents now," Hampton said sadly.

"You're a good agent, Hampton. Don't beat yourself up."

"I was covering for Kilmer, but I really do want a regular field position. I wanted to show that I could take action under pressure."

This explained to Luther why Hampton had left his post in Baltimore and shot one of Luther's attackers.

"You didn't have to prove anything to me," said Luther. "And if it's any consolation, when this is over, no one else will need proof either."

"What Kilmer is doing just doesn't hold water," said Hampton almost to himself. He was confused. The agency had always set the path for him, and now, for the first time, he was on his own. "What are we going to do?"

"We're going to find out what Alex was here for and why Kilmer wants him dead."

"But can we trust a wolf?"

"Alex, Hampton. His name is Alex."

Deavers looked at his old student and invoked that wretched thing he used for a smile.

"You're so much better than I thought," said Alex groggily. "Should I feel proud because I'm a good teacher or sad that I'm no longer the master?"

"Kilmer wanted you dead," said Luther. "Hampton here pretended to kill me, but when the cleanup team comes, they'll know what we did." There were so many other things he wanted to say to his old friend, but right now he had to focus him.

"He did?" said Alex. "That's a surprise. You must know this

man well, Luther. Most people in the agency would've back-washed you without hesitation."

"I'm not most people," said Hampton defiantly. "You've en-dangered all our lives. Tell the man what he wants to know."

"If you refused to kill me," said Deavers, "and you—Hampton, is it?—pretended to execute us both, then Kilmer will send an execution team for all of us."

Luther didn't want to argue with him. He had to keep him talking. "Why would he do that?"

"Because I'm here in Detroit under E-1 Rule 225."

"There *is* no Rule 225," said Luther quickly. "There's—"

"There are only two hundred twenty-four rules in the manual," said Hampton, finishing the thought.

"It's not an official rule, and only us old-timers know of it—and the director, of course," said Alex, adjusting to his bonds in the chair. "Deuce and a Quarter." He laughed. "Ironic."

"I don't see the irony," said Luther.

"My civilian operative, Nappy, was helping me invoke Rule 225, and he drives a car that bears the same number, that's all," said Alex.

Alex sat himself up straight; then as if he were reciting a prayer, he said, " 'When an operative is certain that his agency or the governing body controlling it has been corrupted, the opera-tive shall take all measures necessary to eradicate the corrupting influence and restore justice to all concerned.' That's Rule 225, *my* deuce and a quarter."

"Okay," said Luther to Alex, "if it's true, then what did you learn about the agency to invoke this so-called rule?"

"The murder of the secretary of commerce was a conspiracy," said Alex. "But it had deeper implications than even I knew. I accompanied the secretary to Africa, but my E-1 mission was to recover information from a man named Kiko Salli."

"Kilmer said you were there to kill a strongman named Behiddah," said Luther.

"An internal cover mission," said Alex calmly. "Kilmer had to conceal what he was doing even from his own agents. Behiddah was killed by his own men, just like the news services reported. My mission was to get Salli's information, with the help of the secretary, and then take it from him, replacing it with useless files. The secretary would have knowledge of the information but no proof."

"If Kilmer wanted the secretary dead, why not ask you to do it?" asked Luther.

"First, I wouldn't have done it," said Deavers. "The secretary posed no threat to the United States. Second, I think the decision to kill us all came later. I don't think Kilmer wanted to chance anything. But he picked a man outside E-1, he got sloppy, and I got lucky."

"So where is the information?" asked Luther. He didn't expect Alex to tell him, so this would be the end of the interrogation. Alex would try to get free by telling Luther that he had to take him to the information.

"The information I brought from Africa led me to different places. It was hidden in parts of the cities you followed me to. I hid it in the wall of a garage in the backyard of a drug-supply house in your fair city," said Alex.

"How dangerous is this drug house?" asked Luther.

"It supplies runners, so it's minimum security. It's on a street called St. Aubin near your old home. Nice touch, huh?"

"Is this one of Nappy's places?" asked Luther. He knew that it probably was, and he wasn't happy about the prospect of encountering Nappy again.

"Of course," said Alex. "But he doesn't know. I don't trust Nappy that much."

"Why not just tell me all this?" Luther asked with a little anger in his voice. "Why try to kill me and force me to kill you?"

"I calmly ask you to commit treason, to work against your own agency as a counteragent? And what would you have done?"

"I would have killed you," said Luther, "and then I would have looked into it." He saw Alex's point.

"But this information you refer to," said Hampton, "doesn't it speak for itself?"

"Not completely," said Alex. "Which is why I'm here in Detroit. The last part of it, the verifying part, is here, and only I know where it is. The agency doesn't know that, because they've never seen the Africa information."

"And my family?" Luther made this last statement with resentment.

"Rule 225 does not negate the other rules. I was just trying to win the game. They were forfeit, Luther, but you've obviously taken measures to save them. In the end that's always a mistake."

Luther saw real truth in the face of his old mentor. In a job where lies and half-truths were the norm, only action spoke clearly and without taint and deception. Alex's actions had been honest and unsullied. He'd risked his life and endangered the lives of others to obtain something in this city. He'd gone against the agency to do it, and he'd forced a pursuing agent to doubt his commanders by taking that agent to extremes. Luther was left with no logical choice. He believed Alex. God help him, but he believed that Alex's Rule 225 was real.

And then, from the back of his mind, something rose, a statement he'd heard about rules and their importance. He struggled to remember, because so much had happened to him in the last few weeks.

"Why did you kill Lisa Radcliff, the MI6 agent?"

Alex's face did not change. He took on no sad or guilty look at the mention of Lisa's name. "She didn't believe me," he said simply. "I wanted her to join me, but she didn't go for the story simply by being asked. There are too many lies and layers of deception in our lives. Only the mission speaks the truth. And so I knew I had to use the mission to recruit you to my cause."

"Jesus, he *is* insane," said Hampton.

Luther thought he saw something of humanity in Deavers's eyes—just a flash, a wink of the man inside the agent. Alex had loved Lisa as much as an agent could love, and he had killed her for the greater love of duty.

"Where are you now, Alex?" asked Luther. "What do you need?" He was slipping just a little, showing concern for his friend.

"I must . . . we must get the domestic information, marry it to the African information, and clean out our agency," said Alex calmly.

Alex wasn't going to become human again, thought Luther, at least not right now. He was all business. He'd risked everything to get an ally in this mission, and so Luther's compassion was falling on deaf ears and a closed heart.

"What has the agency done?" Hampton asked. "What is the African information?"

"Are you familiar with the Wells Foundation?" asked Alex.

"It's a think tank," said Hampton. "They're funded partially by

big multinationals and partially by the government, although se-
cretly."

"They drew up the Iraqi war plan about three years before it
happened," said Luther.

"The Wells Foundation has been around since we dropped the
big one on Japan," said Alex. "Our government, as a new world
power, was terrified that it would lose this status, and so we sought
to know the one thing that would ensure that it never happened—
the future."

"You're gonna tell me that these guys at Wells are a bunch of
psychics?" asked Luther.

"They predict trends in world affairs—social, economic, and
political," said Hampton.

"They wanted to look into America's future," said Deavers.
"And so the big brains at Wells began to make predictions based
on data and research and every political and cultural event in
this country, from wars to bad TV. And they saw something
in their crystal ball. They saw the new global economy of the
eighties and nineties, the new radicalism and terrorism from
the world of Islam, and something else that hasn't happened
yet: the coming crises of energy, natural resources, and population growth."

"A think tank in Geneva issued a similar report in 1991,"
Hampton chimed in. "Although it dealt only with Central
Europe, the report said the planet will have a major energy and re-
source crisis in the next hundred years."

"Wells agreed, and they told the government that it had to
head this off," said Alex.

"With alternative forms of energy, deep-sea exploration?"
Luther was trying to guess where this was going.

"Those things were probably in the official report, but answers like that depend on research, genius, and things that can't be controlled. In the secret report, your government was told of a more *direct* way to avoid problems."

And Luther knew it even before Alex said the word. There was only one way to directly get energy and resources for a nation so big, and only one continent big enough to satisfy its needs.

"Africa," said Luther.

"Africa was cited by Wells as the continent with the most untapped potential for resources in the world," said Alex.

"But how would we get it?" asked Hampton. There was alarm in his voice.

"The guys at Wells talked about diplomacy, trade, and even using our own African-Americans to draw lines of commonality in the future."

"But none of these actions are illegal," said Luther. "What actions did Wells advise that were not strictly kosher?"

"Wells came up with a simple plan, the one we've been using since we came to these shores: devastation and acquisition."

"We were going to go to war with Africa?" asked Luther, as if the idea were ridiculous.

"Not viable," said Hampton. "A land war could not be won, and the global community would never support it."

"A covert operation?" said Luther. "But on that scale? How?" The questions poured from his mouth as if he were an eager student.

Alex straightened himself in the chair. A lesser man might have asked to be let go, but Luther knew that Alex would not. Alex had taught Luther never to free a prisoner until he could be trusted.

"They came up with a long-term covert operation, one that would run by itself after a while."

"There is no such thing," said Luther. "An operation needs manpower, direction, supervision—and lots of money. And it could never run without them."

"Oh, my sweet Lord," said Hampton. "It could do *just* that if the mechanism were a living thing."

"He *is* a smart one," said Deavers. Alex smiled again. "Some scientists were sent to work on a way to weaken the continent so that it became dependent on us for assistance, and while we were helping cure the problem we created, we'd take over the country by way of our kindness."

Luther's brow furrowed deeply. What was in his mind was monstrous and evil beyond all logic. "The virus," said Luther. "We planted the AIDS virus in Africa?"

"That's what the information suggests, and even if we didn't, the evidence that we wanted to is there," said Deavers.

"Did the president know?" asked Hampton.

"No," said Alex. "In fact, the African information indicates that Wells went to great lengths to hide it from him and others in power. The main culprits seem to be the corporations and certain members of the military, but they needed government cooperation. And after the problem blew up in their faces, all the companies and government types ran off, leaving the CIA holding the bag."

"What makes you think it's true? What do you know?" asked Hampton.

"The African package contains classified papers," said Alex, "papers that are authentic. One of them is from the CIA, an internal summary on kill ratios. I've checked it out. It was written by a young go-getter in the agency, a hot-shot CIA agent named Kilmer Gray."

Luther reacted to this with dread. If this were true, they were all marked men. Kilmer would do anything to keep a secret of this magnitude.

"Why would our government hold on to something so potentially lethal to it?" asked Luther.

"A man at Wells who suddenly grew a conscience took the information and then split it in half. One half he kept hidden here. The African information left the country with him. It contained the whereabouts of the half he left in this country."

"I suppose this man with a conscience was from my hometown," said Luther.

"Dr. Jay Schrier of Detroit. He escaped to Europe and was eventually found and killed. But he'd already sold the information to Kiko Salli's father by then."

"So why didn't Salli retrieve the American part of the information when they bought the African part from Schrier?"

"The whereabouts of the American package was written in an E-1 code, so they didn't know it existed. But when I saw it, I knew."

"Where is it?" Luther asked. "The last part of the American information?"

Alex laughed. It was a hoarse, sick laugh filled with pain, knowledge, and mocking. "It's in the CIA's old annex building, a structure now used by the local city government."

"You did it," said Hampton. "You raised the terrorism alert. Under the Homeland Security Act, it would now have only minimum security. Damn, that's smart." It was obvious Hampton didn't like Alex, but he did admire his cleverness.

And now Luther understood the seemingly random anti-Arab

actions that had set the city on fire in recent weeks. It was all a
covert diversion, misdirection, while Alex hijacked the rest of
Schrier's American information.

"If you're lying, I'll have to kill you," said Luther.

"We're already dead, all three of us," said Alex. "Don't think
Kilmer will take any chances with this. Even if he believes you're
really dead, he'll send men to kill your Mr. Hampton just to be
sure that he didn't see the proof I've collected."

"We already guessed that," said Luther. "Hampton, look after
our friend until I get back."

"Hey, don't kill anyone," said Hampton. He smiled.

"I won't," said Luther.

Kilmer Gray sat pensively in his office. He thought only a second
before he made several calls and then tapped the keyboard on his
desk quietly.

On the world map at E-1 headquarters in Washington, three
agents' gold specks sprouted red lines that shot across the map and
settled on Detroit.

Wolves

Luther got back to the house in Ferndale later that night. The garage where Alex had left the information was nestled in a war zone, and it had taken Luther three hours to get it. He'd waited, watching drug deals go down, and then slipped into the structure, found the package, and sneaked off undetected.

Luther found Alex still secure in the chair, Hampton sitting across from him looking pensive and scared. Alex was wide awake and waiting. Luther had not stopped to read the information he'd retrieved. He still didn't trust Alex fully and didn't want to open the package outside his presence.

Luther presented the package to Alex, who smiled.

"It's not booby-trapped," said Alex.

"Then open it," said Luther.

Alex struggled against his restraints a little but managed to take off the paper, flip the latch on the box, and open it. He held it back out to Luther.

Luther and Hampton took the box and looked inside. There

were original signed papers, memos, and reports. The first one boasted a cover that read:

WELLS COMMITTEE REPORT
ON ENERGY AND RESOURCES:
THE COMING NEW MILLENNIUM CRISIS IN
OVERPOPULATION AND RESULTANT
RESOURCE SHORTAGE

They took their time going over it. It was there, all of it. The report and supplemental material contained everything except how they'd done it. That had to be part of the American information.

Hampton used his computer to decipher the code left by Dr. Schrier.

"It's authentic, Luther," said Hampton. "It's an old E-1 code, a polynumeric brainchild. Jesus, it's all true."

Luther moved over to Alex and removed his restraints. He then took a few steps back as Alex got to his feet.

"I'll be needing my weapons," said Alex. He gazed at Luther inscrutably.

Luther gave Alex back his weapons and waited a tense moment as Alex put them away.

"We have to go," said Hampton. "The cleanup team will be stopping here first."

"For the last time," said Alex, "Kilmer knows about all of this, so he won't send a cleanup crew. He'll send a death squad to eliminate you and cover his mess."

"He's right," said Luther. "The only way for us to save the agency and our lives is to find the rest of this information."

"Perhaps in *your* case," said Alex.

"The agency doesn't know what we know, so for now we have the upper hand," said Hampton.

Luther took out his Ion and opened it. With a precision tool kit, he removed a GPS tracking device that was installed in his phone. Hampton did the same for the goodie box and all the other equipment and removed any devices used by E-1 to locate an agent.

"I did the same thing to my equipment," said Alex. "Great minds think alike, huh?"

Luther, Alex, and Hampton left the house, got into the Ford, and drove away. Luther didn't need Alex to tell him to head for the inner city. It was the only place they would be safe from the kill team—that is, until the team figured it out. Then it would be a race to see whether the kill team could get to Luther and Alex before they secured Dr. Schrier's domestic information.

"Oh, man," said Hampton, "we're all wolves."

Alex howled like a wolf and laughed. Luther couldn't help but smile.

"So how have you been?" asked Alex, sounding downright normal. "We've been out of touch since you went off after the cutups."

"Cutups?" asked Hampton.

"Terrorists," said Luther. The thought of having a normal conversation with Alex, like two old friends, under the current circumstances, was a little unsettling. Did Alex just expect him to pick up where they'd left off in their relationship? Come on, old pal, forget about the murders, the attempts on your life, and the conspiracy that could change the world as we know it? How about them Tigers?

"I've been busy," said Luther flatly.

And for the first time he realized that he was angry with Alex. Alex was larger than life, and he'd painted himself into a corner. Surely there were other ways he could have done this. But try as he might, Luther couldn't see how Alex could have brought forth what he knew without being killed. E-1 had never given him a chance. They'd tried to backwash him in Africa.

"I understand your anger," said Alex. Then his expression blanked as though he'd flipped a switch inside his head, turned something off. "I can't say for sure if I'm a hundred percent, mentally," he said finally.

"*That's* an understatement," said Hampton.

"You're not qualified to be on this mission," Alex shot back. "A TWA is a glorified computer, a man without the guts to kill. We're trained assassins, so I'll thank you to shut up."

"I could've killed you," said Hampton.

"But you didn't. I would have terminated both of you, and Luther would have, too, in the same situation."

"No I wouldn't," said Luther. "Not anymore."

Alex blinked at this change in his old student. "I see."

"If we take the facility tonight and recover the American information, we might be able to end this thing and stay alive," said Hampton.

"Agreed," said Luther. He realized that he'd assumed Alex's mission or had extended his own. In any event, it was not over.

"And what about your family?" asked Alex. "The kill team will probably use them to lure you out. There'll be a fire at the house, or someone will get shot in a drive-by or a car accident. You know the procedure."

Luther had not thought about this fact. They would threaten his family in order to draw him out or make him surrender. He had no choice this time. If E-1 were corrupt in this matter, he had to save his family from them. He didn't care about the rules anymore. He was making up his own.

"We have to ensure that doesn't happen," said Hampton before Luther could.

"If we protect your family, it increases the chance that we'll fail," said Alex calmly.

"Can we take the facility right away?" asked Luther, ignoring Alex's grim prediction.

"Yes," said Alex. "I've been working on it since I got here. We'll have to take the place quickly, so some of the guards might have to be neutralized."

"No," said Luther.

"We can't afford to get self-righteous," said Alex. "Getting the information is all that matters now."

"I don't work for you," said Luther.

"If your Rule 225 exists," said Hampton, "then we all work for the people of this country."

"You want to take on an E-1 kill team, protect your family, *and* retrieve the information—all without anyone dying?" asked Alex.

"I didn't say that," said Luther. "I just don't think our normal method of kill first should be employed anymore."

"Sounds nice and humane," said Alex, "but the cleanup team will be here, and the first thing they'll do is go after your family. How are we going to get the information and guard them at the same time?"

"I'm surprised at you," said Luther. "Surely you know that when an agent is faced with the impossible, he's expected to win. And the first way to win in an impossible situation is to employ the very elements that created it."

"I can't believe you remembered that," said Alex.

"I did, and it's what we're going to do," said Luther.

"How?" asked Alex.

"I don't know," said Luther. "My TWA is a certified genius, and I'm sure he'll come up with a way."

"No pressure there," said Hampton. "Okay, I can think of several ways to approach this. We can tell your family what you do for a living and hope they believe it."

"They wouldn't believe it," said Luther. "Maybe we can just ask them to evacuate."

"Possibly," said Hampton. "Do you think we can get them all together?"

"They're at my mother's place today for a family meeting," said Luther.

"We should leave them and continue the mission," said Alex. "If they die, so be it."

"I'd expect that from you, since you already tried to blow them all to hell. . . ." Luther stopped for a moment, then smiled. "I got it," he said.

Kill Team

Frank Hedgispeth watched the Green house from a street over. He sat in a dark van that was backed into a vacant lot and pointed at the house, peering through high-powered binoculars. Next to him was a sniper's rifle.

He hadn't seen Luther since he'd left D.C. When they hit town to take out Hampton, they had found the safe house empty and no evidence of the double kill he'd reported. That meant that Luther and Alex Deavers were still alive. Three wolves. A career-making opportunity.

Kilmer wasn't about to take Hampton's word for what he'd heard over the phone, so he'd called Frank, who was shocked at being given the green light to take out Luther, Hampton, and any captive they held.

Luther had fallen for Alex Deavers's bullshit, and now he would pay for it. And he'd done it in his hometown, making Rule 35 applicable. Surely Luther would know they'd go after his family to lure him into the open. Luther had never spoken much of his family, and so Frank figured that he didn't care about them. Kilmer assured him that this was not so, and therefore they would proceed as normal. Frank had made a critical decision in this regard. He'd decided to terminate one of Luther's family members to let him know they were serious.

But which one? thought Frank. Not the mother. Even an E-1 agent wasn't that low, although taking her would certainly elicit a stronger response. No, he was thinking about the father or maybe an older brother. Those were relationships that hit a man hard as well.

Frank was the leader of this operation. He didn't want to use the term "kill team," but that was their mission. They were to bring Alex and Luther back to E-1 neutralized. It wouldn't be easy. Alex was a master, and Luther, Frank had to admit, was formidable as well. This would be a great thing for him, he thought. Completing this mission would put him at the top of Kilmer's list, and he would get rid of a rival in the process. Frank had planned to be director of E-1 in ten years. He had just lowered that number to seven.

Sharon Bane walked up and stood next to the car. She had not talked much since arriving in Detroit. Frank knew that she didn't share his zeal for this mission. In fact, Kilmer had told him that Sharon's friendship with Luther made her a liability, but she knew him better than anyone else and could be of use.

"How long until we make our move?" Sharon asked.

"I'm thinking another hour or so," said Frank. "I've decided to take the father."

"Okay, but we'll still need a backup."

"Big brother," said Frank calmly.

Frank's radio crackled, and he switched it on quickly. "Yes."

"Still nothing back here," said Kam Lim over the radio. Kam was the third agent assigned to the mission, watching the back of the house. He'd been on assignment in San Francisco when he was called in. Kam was a ruthless agent, known to dislike Luther ever since the latter had injured him in a martial arts tournament.

"We're going to move in one hour," said Frank. "If anyone comes your way, you know what to do."

"Right," said Kam. "But if that happens, we have to take them all, right?" Kam could not hide the eagerness in his voice. Sharon shook her head in disapproval. Even Frank didn't like it.

"That will be on my order only," said Frank.

"Sure thing," said Kam, forcing his voice back into a respectful mission tone. He obviously knew he'd gone too far. "Who's our target acquisition?"

"The father," said Frank.

Kam acknowledged the target and signed off. Frank heaved a small sigh and turned off the radio. Sharon climbed into the car and settled next to Frank.

"I don't know why Kilmer would send Kam Lim on this mission," she said. "He harbors some personal animosity against the wolf since that incident in training."

Frank was glad to hear Sharon refer to Luther as a wolf. She had depersonalized him, and that meant she would take him out on sight.

"I wouldn't have," said Frank, "but Kilmer's the boss, and maybe things are different when you're in charge."

"I can't believe Luther did this," said Sharon. "It's the dumbest thing he's ever done."

"I don't get it either. All I can think of is that Alex Deavers is really good."

"I wonder how Deavers turned him," Bane wondered.

"Who knows?" said Frank. "Not our job to wonder why."

"So what did Kilmer mean when he said for us to neutralize the wolves and destroy all property possessed by them? That was a very unusual request."

"Again, I didn't ask," said Frank. "We got three wolves, Sharon. When this is over, we should talk about your future."

Frank felt Sharon stiffen next to him. She knew he liked her, and it was rather inappropriate to get into personal matters on assignment.

"This mission will put us both in the limelight," Frank continued. "And you need to think about where you want to be when the fieldwork is over. I mean, you don't want to be punching security buttons like Adelaide, do you?"

"I never thought about it," said Sharon. "And for the record, I like Adelaide."

"You know what I mean."

"I do," said Sharon. "And I've already decided that I don't want to become some D.C. lobbyist or an agency head. I'm going to retire noncom, take the money, and start a business—a little restaurant back home."

"Bullshit," said Frank. "You like the action. You'll be in the trenches with me."

"Don't count on it," said Sharon. "When this is all over, I want to go back to being a normal human being."

"I didn't think anyone ever did that," said Frank.

"Then I'll be the first."

"You know, Kilmer didn't want to send you. I lobbied for you."

"Why didn't he want me?"

"Opposite reason from Kam. He thought you liked Luther too much."

"He's wrong about that. I'll pull the trigger on him, no hesitation," said Sharon without emotion.

The first police siren sounded distantly and did not cause any of the kill team concern. But then they heard another; then a fire truck and an ambulance siren followed. The first ones sounded from the east, then the south, and then they were coming from all around. The police, fire department, and paramedics were headed toward something very nearby. It didn't take Frank long to see that the multitude of emergency vehicles were closing in on the area containing the Green house.

Luther drove Alex away from the east side into downtown. Luther carried a sleek tranquilizer gun.

"You really planning to use that thing?" asked Alex.

"Whenever necessary," said Luther. "If we get in and out of this place quickly, maybe I won't have to."

"You sure your TWA doesn't mind baby-sitting your family?" asked Alex.

"He didn't complain," said Luther.

Alex smiled proudly. "You wouldn't have caught me if he hadn't helped you, you know."

"I know," said Luther.

"We'll have to go into the building next door first," said Alex. "It'll be easy because it's uninhabited. From there we'll access the lower level. There should be an old exit door leading to the target building. We can get in through that."

Luther turned on the CD player and chose a nasty rap tune by

L'il John and the Ying Yang Twins. The thick bass filled the cab of the truck. He was in a new state of mission mode now. Before, he'd had a mind that swept away reason and emotion. Now he was focused, and although violence was certain, it was not desired.

"I prefer the Stones myself," said Alex. "But this is nice, too."

Luther pulled the Ford onto Randolph Street, and then they rolled into a nearby alley. Luther took out a perfect forgery of a city parking permit and placed it on the windshield.

Around them the city chugged along, oblivious to the coming storm. Luther and Alex checked their equipment and then moved toward the access building.

They easily broke into the first building, an abandoned edifice that sat on Randolph Street. The city was slowly rebuilding, but there were still many great old buildings that stood empty. The one that they'd just entered had once been dominated by offices that had belonged to Packard Motors.

Next to it was the target, the Wall Building, which used to house several law firms but was now a secure storage facility for the city of Detroit. Sensitive police files and city-government documents were warehoused there. There was even a historical-documents room filled with priceless treasures, from the private papers of past mayors and governors to the territorial charter of the French colony that had founded the city.

The normally tight security had been relaxed, thanks to Alex's hard work. Now there were only six guards in the entire building.

Luther and Alex moved into the dark basement. It was a large space but so pitch-black inside that they needed flashlights to illuminate the way.

"Southeast corner," said Alex. "That's where the exit is."

The wolves headed in that direction until they heard movement behind them. Luther immediately turned with his tranq gun pulled. He saw nothing. Then he heard the sound again, a thick rustling of the trash and wood on the floor. He scanned his light downward and saw something moving in the debris. He waited, both he and Alex standing perfectly still. Then the thing on the floor came closer to them. Luther saw some old newsprint move and fired into it. The tranq gun hardly made a sound as it shot a small silver stiletto into whatever the thing was. Luther waited a moment for more movement and then approached the mass. He cleared away the paper and found a large rat underneath. It was out cold, its jagged teeth bared and its red eyes still open.

"That's one enemy down," said Alex.

"At least I know the gun works," said Luther.

They moved on and were soon at the southern wall, a tall gray-brick roadblock that looked as solid now as the day it was made.

"How do we find the exit?" said Luther.

"The old CIA exits were manual," said Alex. "If it's sealed, we'll have to break through it."

"Let's find a loose brick, then work our way around it. That way we won't make a lot of noise."

They searched the wall and in the bottom left corner found a loose set of bricks. Thick cable ran through them, and soon they were able to discern that it was a door that could be lifted from the other side. Alex and Luther worked for an hour dislodging the bricks, until there was nothing left but the iron cable door. They easily pushed it in.

When they got into the other building, they realized that the area was still in good shape. There were the remnants of an exit room, complete with empty weapons ports. Above them they heard footfalls and activity.

"They keep a skeleton crew here on the weekends," said Alex. "They only have about three or four guys, one of whom is security. Normally there would be three cops outside and two on the inside, but my terror alert has shifted them away."

"Good," said Luther. "There's a staircase. Where do we need to go once we're inside?"

"The papers are hidden in a wall in the northeast corner," said Alex. "We'll have to travel a long way. The walls are standard issue, so one of us can hold off any security threat and the other can access the wall and the information. But there's one trick: Schrier laid a trap, and if I don't approach the package just right and lift it from its foundation gently, I'll destroy what I came to get."

"You retrieve the information," said Luther. "I'll handle the rest."

The old CIA exit chamber had a single staircase that rose to the ground-floor level. Luther and Alex ascended the staircase slowly. The plan was that Luther would rush into the main file room and hold the workers and any security at bay while Alex found the information. Luther went up first, hoping that no one gave him any trouble.

Frank knew they had a problem when the first police cars stopped on the street. The cops in the cruisers looked alert and a little scared. They emerged with weapons drawn and talked urgently into radios.

Maybe it was a drug takedown, Frank thought, just more urban violence that would soon pass. If that was the case, then all they would have to do was wait. Patience was one of the first things they'd learned at E-1. A good agent could wait you to death.

But soon a fire truck and an ambulance settled in, and then more cops came, this time detectives. Helicopters were heard overhead. By the time the first FBI car arrived, Frank knew that something major was going on, and it wasn't good for his mission.

"What the hell is it?" asked Sharon Bane.

"Don't know," said Frank. "I was hoping that it was a drug bust, but I don't think so."

"The police band is really humming," said Sharon. "Turn it up."

Frank was about to when Kam called in and reported that the same activity was occurring on the streets behind the house. He would have to get out soon, or he'd be hemmed in.

Frank cursed loudly. He told Kam to hold tight, and then he tuned in the police band and heard the report of what was going down. A terror alert had been declared in Detroit. Frank knew this but had made no connection between it and his mission.

There was a report of a bomb in the area. A tip had come in earlier that day. Frank burned with anger as he saw a unit of the police bomb squad roll in and begin to search close to the Green house. It was a setup, he thought, a brilliant move by Luther to protect his family. The police went to every occupied house on the block and began to evacuate families.

"That sonofabitch," said Sharon.

"He hasn't won this round yet," said Frank. "I can still get one of them on their way out."

"But if you shoot one of them," said Sharon, "the rest of them will be kept in protective custody."

"And if I don't, Luther wins," said Frank. "This way he'll at least get our message. He'll know he has to deal or we'll take out the rest of them. And the cops won't know why one of them was killed. They'll say it was a local criminal, or maybe terror-related."

"Maybe," said Sharon. "But it reeks of desperation."

Frank called Kam in. Kam gladly got out of his position, moved back to his vehicle, and easily slipped through the tightening police net.

He raised his sniper's rifle and trained it on the front door to the Green house. As soon as he saw movement, he would take out the first person to come through the door.

Luther pushed his way through the old trapdoor in the floor of the city records building. He rose up and took position while Alex came through. The space was large and filled with high rows of old files. Luther slowly moved through the stacks to his left, and Alex went in the opposite direction. Luther had heard voices and crept around behind them to get a better look. He took out his radio and pointed to it. Alex immediately took out a similar radio and moved on.

Luther moved row by row until he could just see the men who worked in the facility. He raised the tranquilizer gun and was about to shoot when he saw the familiar nondescript suits favored by feds. Two men were talking to the workers, who wore blue jumpsuits. There was no sign of any security guard. The two feds wore shades and seemed to be asking questions. Luther wasn't sure what agency they were with but his gut told him CIA.

"Agency's here," said Luther into his radio in a very low voice.

"E-1?" asked Alex just as quietly.

"Don't think so. I'd guess CIA, but only two," said Luther. "I think your terror alert has come back to bite us in the ass. There's probably a directive to check all old and new facilities."

"Kilmer," said Alex. "He's desperate."

"And smart," said Luther.

"I'm at the wall," said Alex. "Take them."

Luther lowered the radio and raised the tranq gun again. He had it trained on the bigger of the two agents, who wore a gray suit, when he felt someone behind him.

Luther turned and raised a foot into the face of a security guard, who'd been in the men's room. Luther's foot connected with his jaw, and he dropped. As the man was falling, Luther pumped a tranquilizer dart into his chest. He was out before he hit the floor. Luther had to move. The noise would have alerted the agents. He ran several stacks over, keeping low. Then he heard a door open and footsteps as the two file room workers left the room. Luther didn't have much time. He had to take them now.

He moved away from Alex, making noise and hoping that this would buy some time. He went another few stacks over, but he sensed only one man following his movement. Where was the other agent? Had he discovered Alex? Luther didn't hear any gunfire or fighting, so he assumed that this was not the case. Still, he'd lost the second agent and didn't know how. He kept moving. Soon he'd run out of room, and they would have him.

Luther wanted to take out the big guy first but couldn't tell which shadowy figure he was. Then he caught a glimpse of someone in an open space in a midlevel shelf two stacks over. It was the other agent, the smaller one, who wore a blue suit.

If Luther was quick, he could catch the man as he came

around the end of the row. He would be at a distance, but he could take him. Luther moved to the end of his row and ran toward the advancing figure. Luther shot him in the neck with a dart, and the man fell on his face.

Luther sensed the other man above him before he could make his move. The big agent had climbed onto the top of a row and was moving parallel to his partner, a brilliant tactic that made him seem as if he were gone from the chase. Luther lunged into the metal shelf, and the CIA agent fired a shot that missed. The stack tilted, and the man fell. He was agile enough to land on his feet, but not without dropping his weapon. Before Luther could hit him with a dart, the CIA man kicked the tranq gun from his hand.

The two men faced each other. The agent attacked swiftly, with a kick that just missed. Luther threw a backhand punch that was wide, and he paid for it when the agent spun low and hit him in the back. Luther recovered and turned to face his nemesis. The agent attacked again and hit Luther with a combination of punches that brought him to his knees. Then the agent made the mistake of trying to finish Luther off with his gun. He leaped to retrieve it, but by the time he had his hand on it, Luther was on him. First Luther kicked the gun away and with the same foot kicked the agent in the face. The agent rolled backward and attempted to get to his feet, but Luther had taken a stride and sent a side kick that lifted the agent into the air and slammed him into a wall. Luther quickly ran back and got his tranquilizer gun, shooting the agent before he could recover.

Luther then ran to the northeast corner of the place to see how Alex was doing. When he got there, he saw a hole at the base of the wall. Whatever had been there was gone.

And so was Alex.

Luther heard a noise from the front of the room, and then he remembered the two file-room workers. He raced to the back of the place and climbed into the little door hidden in the floor. Luther moved down the old exit into the basement, across to the new building, then out. They would probably find the exit, but it wouldn't matter.

Luther walked out of the abandoned building and then ran to his Ford, which was still parked in the alley. But when he got there, he found no sign of Alex. He was gone.

Luther cursed silently. What was he up to now? Luther was about to climb into the Ford when he saw a police cruiser roll into the alley.

"Police!" said a voice over the car's speaker system. "Stop right there!"

The police dispersed the crowd that was trying to form on the street where the Green house was located. People from the surrounding neighborhood had seen or heard the commotion and came out of their houses in droves. The local news stations were also there in force, and at least one news copter was circling the event.

Frank still had a clear shot at the Green house two streets away. The police had secured that street and the next one over. They were between him and his target, but he could still get the kill if he wanted.

Frank breathed evenly as he waited for the police to make their way to the Green house. Someone inside had already come to the door to see what the commotion was about but was told by a police officer to go back in. It was clear that the FBI was leading this exercise, but the local cops were arrogant and determined to have some measure of authority.

"What the hell are they waiting for?" said Frank.

"They have to find the bomb," said Kam, who had doubled back and joined them.

"There's no bomb," said Frank. "It's a hoax designed to stall us, but Luther should've known better. When they come out of that house, I'll take the first face I see."

"There's a bomb," said Sharon. "Luther wouldn't engage in this kind of major distraction if there wasn't a real threat. It defeats his purpose."

"Makes sense," Kam joined in. "If nothing else, Green is thorough."

Frank argued with them until a young cop on the bomb squad yelled to his team that he'd found something. In the backseat of an abandoned car, right next door to the Green house, was an explosive device. This information came over the local police band. The already high tension soared even higher. The crowd backed away en masse, and the police intensified the evacuation process.

"We should pack it in," said Sharon.

"No," said Frank. "I still have a shot."

"We can't risk it this close to the action," said Sharon. "You make a kill in this atmosphere, and we'll be exposed. There's a helicopter up there."

"I'd take the shot," said Kam.

"You would," said Sharon.

"What the fuck is that supposed to mean?" Kam demanded angrily.

"It means that your personal feelings about the wolf are not appreciated here," said Sharon.

"Me?" said Kam. "You're his best buddy. If anyone is con-flicted, it's you, lady."

Sharon turned on Kam, looking murderous. She hated the im-plication that she was not professional, but even more than that, she didn't like being called "lady."

"Enough," said Frank. "It's my mission to lead, and I'm taking the shot."

The officers on the bomb squad related the news, and the offi-cers working crowd control moved any remaining spectators away. Another group continued to empty each house of its occu-pants. Soon a team of cops walked to the Green house. They stood in the doorway as the shocked family members moved to-ward the door.

Mary came out first.

She looked scared as she emerged from the house into the bright sun. Frank settled the crosshairs on her head and squeezed the trigger.

Luther froze as the cops got out of the police cruiser. In the front of the building, more police poured in. Luther carried a bag with equipment in it and was dirty from being in the basement. He could take them easily, but he felt there might not be any need.

"What's going on, Officers?" he asked. One of the cops checked the city sticker on his Ford while the other approached him, hand on his sidearm.

"We got a problem next door," said a young black officer.

"What kind of problem?" Luther sounded scared.

"Nothing to worry about," said the black cop. "What are you doing here?"

"Well, I got a problem in this building," said Luther. "Damned thing's falling down. Scheduled for demolition, but it's so close to this other place that we're going to have to collapse it. That's where we level the far side and let it fall on itself away from the other structure. See, we do that by—"

"He's got a city inspector's sticker," said the other cop, a plump white woman.

"You need ID or something?" asked Luther.

The black cop thought for only a moment, then said, "Have you seen anything unusual in the last hour or so?"

"Nope, just big-ass rats in the basement," said Luther.

"You'd better get out of here," said the cop.

Luther smiled and complied. He got into the Ford and drove away. He'd succeeded in not killing anyone, but he'd lost Alex.

Mary Green stepped onto the stone porch of her mother's house. She was scared and didn't like the way the police were yelling at everyone. She raised her hand to brush some hair out of her face. The bracelet on her arm caught the sun and reflected it with a glare back into the morning.

Frank Hedgispeth caught a blinding flash of light in his scope as he squeezed the trigger. The reflection from Mary Green's bracelet threw off his aim, and his shot missed by inches, hitting the forward wall of the Green house.

The cops yanked Mary to the ground and pulled out their weapons, looking around. The agitated atmosphere on the street grew even more intense as the Green family was ushered out of the house under police guard and into an FBI van. Since the bomb had been found next to their house, they would all be interrogated about anything suspicious.

In the van Frank was cursing loudly. He'd missed a clear shot. The cops were now all turning and pointing in his direction.

The van's engine started, and Frank felt it lurch forward. He didn't complain as Sharon pulled away from the scene as fast as she could. They easily escaped the scene before the cops found their empty lot.

Conspiracy Theory

Luther had listened to the news report on the bomb threat outside his mother's house. This meant that his family was in custody, probably federal custody. Hampton had used Alex's covert misdirection of anti-Arab sentiment and domestic terrorism against the kill team. They had even rewired Alex's homemade bomb, careful to take off the BEP logo so that no one could trace it back to E-1.

There was a report that a shot had been fired at the bomb location, but it was unconfirmed. Luther knew that the kill team had taken that shot. Why they had missed was a mystery.

The other mystery was why Alex had run. Was the whole thing some kind of scam? No, Luther told himself, the African information was authentic, and, moreover, Luther still had it. Alex's information was no good without it. Still, it wasn't like Alex to panic.

Suddenly Luther's short-range radio sounded. He immediately lifted it and spoke.

"Alex?" he said urgently. "Where are you?"

"That's not important," said Alex. The connection was very clear, and since the radios had a limited range, it meant that Alex was close by. Luther pulled the Ford over on Griswold Street and waited. It was illegal to park there, but he'd stay as long as he could. Alex was somewhere downtown.

"I can pick you up," said Luther.

"No need," said Alex. "I won't be coming back. You have to complete this mission without me. The package is in the rear of your vehicle under the mat. Did you know that Rule 225 is derived from something Abraham Lincoln said?"

"No, I didn't."

"I'm sure I'll meet Lincoln one day." Alex waited a moment, then said, "I hope your family is safe." With that he signed off.

Luther quickly went into the back of the Ford and found the package Alex had retrieved from the building. This was the last part of Schrier's domestic information. Along with the Africa portion, Luther now had the entire conspiracy in his hands. He guessed that Alex didn't want any more of the risk now that the mission was done. His mental stability was highly questionable. It was probably better that he go. Luther had the mantle now, and he would see that the information was used properly.

He got back into the Ford and drove away, headed for the inner city. He and Hampton had a prearranged place to meet. The kill team knew he was still alive, and they'd be out looking for him.

Was Alex going to try to take out five or six E-1 agents by himself? He'd probably fail, but it was standard procedure. An attack was the one thing they would not expect. Luther didn't know what he would do about that right now, but he did know that he had to read both sets of documents in order to finally understand just what he was up against.

Luther drove to a little neighborhood just south of the Davison Freeway on the east side, adjacent to Highland Park. He found Hampton waiting for him there in his car. Looking a little shaken, Hampton climbed into the Ford.

"Where's Deavers?" he asked.

"He left," said Luther.

"Goddamn it! That bastard, I should have shot him—"

"He left me the information, Hampton."

"Oh . . . but why did he . . . ? Well, I guess that's okay." Hampton calmed down. "What is he going to do?"

"I think he's going to try to take out the kill team."

"God be with him. So how many casualties did you have?"

"None," said Luther, smiling. "I think it's time we read all this stuff and find out just what the hell Kilmer's hiding."

Luther and Hampton put together all the information they'd collected. It had to be decoded and then read in order, but eventually the whole story emerged.

Dr. Jay Schrier had been one of Wells's most trusted members. He had assisted the think tank in every endeavor, legal and illegal, over the seven years he'd worked there. Then his daughter became ill and died of leukemia. This changed everything for Dr. Schrier. He found religion and grew to dislike what his bosses were doing. When the Africa project was dreamed up by military and corporate types, he became deeply angry. There were so many good things they could be doing, and they'd chosen to decimate an entire continent.

The two sets of documents verified a plan to subvert and acquire major parts of Africa over the next half century. A large portion of this plan consisted of disabling the population and allow the United States to come in with an aid package as a cover for land acquisitions through governments they could control.

The scientific documents were the most damning of all. Even a layman could understand the procedure that had been used and how it was systematically implemented. Names and dates were given, verifiable incidents recounted. Five major U.S. corporations knew about the project, along with certain high-level members of the Defense Department and, of course, the CIA.

What the information suggested was a nightmare, a crime monstrous enough to rival the greatest atrocities in the annals of history. Both parts of the package showed a scientific summary of how they'd done it. There was a lot of medical and technical detail, but the basic story told of two viruses, SIV and HIV. The former occurs in monkeys and does not harm humans. That 1 percent difference in our DNA makes humans immune to SIV. SIV is the older virus, and so it was assumed that HIV was a mutant form, but scientists could not figure out how it had mutated. That's why the myth of a man having sex with a monkey had surfaced, thought Luther.

In reality the Wells people had found a procedure for mutating SIV. It was unstable, but they'd managed to infect a control group, then had that group infect a second group, then another and another. And all the time the ruthlessly efficient bastards had kept killing the prior group until there was no trace of the lab mutation.

And then it got away from them.

It was supposed to be a controlled kill, a self-running, long-term, covert operation. But they fucked up. One of the generational mutated viruses got loose, and the whole thing went to hell.

Luther and Hampton finished their reading. It was all there. Kilmer had been a big proponent of the plan, along with several others from the military, the government, and big business. The group as a whole was referred to from time to time by Kilmer as the APG—Africa Project Group. They were resolute in their mission, and anyone who opposed them had been bought off or had just conveniently disappeared.

Hampton pulled out his laptop and a handheld scanner and quickly copied all the information into a file. Then he packed up both halves of the package.

"I'm going to call Kilmer and tell him what we have," Luther announced.

"Why?" asked Hampton. "Let's just go to the White House. We'll both live longer."

"But Kilmer has to deal. Even though the conspiracy was not completely government-backed, there were enough ties to embarrass the U.S. for decades and ensure a weakened global authority—not to mention the domestic impact."

"I see your point. Political careers will be lost, special prosecutors assigned."

"History will change," said Luther.

"What about the kill team? What will Kilmer do with them?"

"I don't know. They need to watch their backs with Alex out there. I'd warn them, but then again they did come to assassinate us."

Luther took out his Ion. He hadn't used it since he'd removed the tracking device. He was about to dial when he thought of something.

"Hampton, E-1 has known every place I've been since I hit town, right?"

"I would say so, yes."

"And the kill team failed in the hit on my family. . . ."

Luther started the Ford and roared off. Hampton was thrown back in the seat as they tore onto the Davison Freeway.

"What the hell . . . ?"

"The kill team will go to any Rule 35 backup they can find."

"What backup? Your whole family was there in the house," said Hampton.

"Not everyone," said Luther. "You've made reports on everything, right?"

"Yes."

"Then E-1 knows every contact I've made," said Luther. "All of them."

Dr. Vanessa Brown was ending a good day. She had seen great progress on two patients, and a third, a little girl with a nasty virus, was looking good as well. It was days like this when she remembered why she'd gone through hell to become a physician.

Her offices were on the ninth floor of a high-rise in Southfield near Ten Mile Road. It was a modern building with a private parking area for VIP tenants. Dr. Brown qualified for this special treatment because she was leasing almost half the ninth floor. Business was very good. There were not many general practitioners left in the medical business, so she was a popular woman.

Vanessa was thinking about Luther as she finished up with her last patients. He wasn't the old Luther anymore; he was different, almost like he'd become someone else.

Luther had been destined for great things. She'd always seen him as an international businessman or maybe a politician. But she didn't know what he really did for a living. His "government contractor" story was thin, and he always seemed to be hiding something. She wondered what his life had been like for the last decade, where he'd been and whom he'd been with.

"You're double-booked again," said Deena Wilson, Vanessa's office manager and part-time medical assistant.

"You know the drill. Put them in adjacent rooms and give me both files."

"Hiring another doctor would solve this problem, you know," said Deena with a sly smile.

This was a conversation they'd had many times. Vanessa had interviewed many potential medical partners, and she'd always found something wrong with them. They were too serious, not serious enough, too Republican, too "technical." In reality Vanessa just didn't like to give her precious patients to another doctor.

"Don't start, Deena," said Vanessa. "Just get the other patient ready."

"Yes, ma'am."

Deena walked off. Vanessa smiled and moved on to her next patient, happy to be ending her day on a good note. Her thoughts again went to Luther. She wondered why he'd really come back home and if she'd see him again.

"Doctor, there's a man here to see you," said Deena.

"We're almost done for the day," said Vanessa.

"He says he's from the FBI."

Vanessa sighed, then walked to the waiting area. There she saw a man seated on a couch reading one of her many magazines. He was alone—all her other patients were in examining rooms.

"May I help you?" asked Vanessa.

The man didn't respond. He pulled open his jacket, revealing a gun.

The kill team arrived at the medical center just before Dr. Vanessa Brown was scheduled to come down. Frank drove the van toward the building and around to the back. They planned to gain access through the service area and take Dr. Brown in the building's underground parking lot. Sharon wanted to wait and take the doctor at her home, but Frank had vetoed that. He didn't want to wait and he had a feeling that Luther would have taken steps to protect Dr. Brown at her home.

Hampton had reported that Luther had contacted this Dr. Brown only once, but a check of his E-1 file showed that she was an old flame from high school. The agency's background check was thorough, and it was at times like these that Frank was glad they did it. Brown obviously meant something to Luther, and maybe this would give them an advantage. Frank thought it was totally out of character for Luther to have such a soft spot. It would prove his undoing.

Frank's mission was simple: They would kill this Dr. Brown and then move on.

The kill team went to the rear of the building. There were supposed to be posted guards, but they didn't see any.

"Did you check the security rotation?" Frank asked Kam Lim.

"Yes," said Kam. "It's—"

Suddenly their van was hit by two quick shots. Frank, Sharon, and Kam all armed themselves as Frank pulled the van to a stop.

Luther stood in the service door of the building holding a weapon. Quick as a flash, he was gone.

"He wants us to follow," said Sharon.

"Then it's got to be a trap," said Kam.

"I know," said Frank. "He's diverting us from the girl, this Dr. Brown."

"Your call," said Sharon.

"We didn't come here to kill some doctor. Let's take him."

Hampton hustled Vanessa, her staff, and the last few patients out of the offices and down to their cars. He sighed in relief after they were all safely away. He'd told them that he was FBI, that the terror threat had come to the suburbs, and that this building had to be cleared out. No one had questioned him.

Hampton checked his watch. If all were going well, Luther would need him soon.

Frank and his team opened the door to the rooftop of the building, having followed Luther up there. Luther wanted a show-down, and Frank planned to give him one. The kill team had put on flak jackets. Kam carried a Namor autogun. Frank and Sharon held 9mm pistols.

It was windy as they stepped out of the service stairway. The sun was setting, and its orange-gold rays washed over the rooftop. Bane and Kam Lim took flanking positions around Frank.

There were tall power stations angled and lined up on one side of the roof. The way they were positioned, a man would be hard to see as long as he kept behind them in the proper angle. The sun was in their eyes as well, thought Frank. Luther was a clever adversary indeed.

"The power stations," said Frank. "Spread out. As soon as he shows himself, we take him."

"Wait," said Sharon. She went to the stairwell door, closed it, then stuck a small device on it. If someone opened the door, he would get blown away.

Sharon joined her partners, and then the three agents dispersed, fanning out in an arc and moving almost in unison along the line of the power stations.

Luther saw them enter the roof area from the stairwell. He was behind one of the first power stations. As they walked closer, he quickly stepped to the next one, knowing that all they might catch was a glimpse of him.

Luther had the sun at his back, so they would have an even harder time seeing him. He was playing a dangerous game.

The kill team arced out as they approached. Kam Lim was the closest to him. Since Kam was the best fighter of the three, he would have to go first. Luther pulled on a pair of dark goggles and waited.

Without warning, the door to the stairwell was blown off its hinges and went sailing across the concrete roof. Kam Lim jumped up as it skidded under his feet.

Sharon turned her weapon at the now open stairwell. Kam and Frank kept their eyes on the power stations.

"I don't see anyone!" said Sharon.

"Dammit!" yelled Frank. "The explosion will bring the locals. Let's—"

Just then a small black disk flew from the dark stairwell, over Sharon's head. As it hit the ground, it burst into brilliant light.

The kill team was momentarily blinded. Luther rushed to Kam and slammed a blow into Kam's neck. Kam dropped his Namor, swung, and connected to Luther's chest. Luther grabbed Kam's arm and spun his body around between him and the rest of the kill team. Then he shot Kam with the tranq gun and ran off back toward the power stations as Kam fell into a heap on the ground.

The light faded. Frank and Sharon saw Kam's body. Frank checked him and then cursed as he scanned the area, looking for his prey.

"He's hiding there," said Frank to Sharon, indicating the power stations.

Sharon ran to the stairwell and ripped several shots down the stairs.

"Forget him!" said Frank.

Sharon ran back to Frank, not wanting to take her eyes off the stairwell.

Frank and Sharon moved in tandem to each of the stations, and then Frank walked to the back of the first one so that he and Sharon kept the stations between them as they moved along. If Luther was hiding, he'd be flushed out.

One by one the stations passed between them. Sharon kept looking back at the stairwell, fearful that Hampton or Alex Deavers or whoever it was might still be there.

As they approached the end of the long row, Luther struck. He leaped from behind a station, grabbed Sharon's gun, and raised it up. She fired into the air. Luther hit Sharon with a blow to the jaw, then grabbed her twisting body and wrenched her gun away from her.

Frank stepped clear of the station and found Luther hidden behind Sharon. He froze for just an instant, but it was long enough for Luther to thrust Sharon at him. They fell into each other. Frank's gun was dislodged from his hand and skidded across the concrete floor.

Frank and Sharon recovered and moved to attack. Sharon jump-kicked at Luther, but he sidestepped her. Unfortunately, his movement sent him too close to Frank, who caught him with a glancing blow. Luther recovered, then grabbed Frank's arm. He paid dearly for this as Frank reversed the hold and drove an elbow into his side. Before Frank could strike again, Luther dropped and swept Frank's legs from under him, rising just in time to avoid Sharon's side kick.

Luther went to Frank and grabbed him. Sharon was advancing again, and Luther used Frank to block her. He pushed Frank into her, pushing Frank's elbow into her jaw. They both toppled, then scrambled back to their feet.

Luther moved quickly to Frank and kicked him in the temple, knocking him out. He turned to Sharon and was ready to finish her, but he stopped cold. In her hand was a gun. In that instant Luther thought that she must have recovered it when he pushed them to the floor.

Luther raised the tranq gun, and they both fired at the same time. Luther was hit in the upper right chest and fell backward. The tranq gun's dart hit Sharon in the neck. She was out before she made contact with the floor.

Luther struggled to his feet. He was badly hit, but he still had one good arm, which he used to shoot Frank with a tranq dart.

Luther then went to the stairwell and called down to Hampton. Hampton answered. He was down a few levels, waiting, and he quickly ran up to the roof. "You okay?" he asked.

"Barely," said Luther. "Did they get out all right?" he asked, referring to Vanessa and her staff.

"They're fine," said Hampton. "Long gone. Goddamned bomb on the door was smart. Luckily I'm smarter. I triggered it with a minicharge of my own."

"Guess I'll have to find a new TWA," said Luther.

"This is bad," said Hampton, pointing to Luther's wound. "We need to get you out of here."

Hampton dressed Luther's arm as fast as he could, and then they began the long process of dragging their three captives away.

Spook

Kilmer Gray was worried. The kill team had checked in last night, but Agent Hedgispeth had not called Kilmer directly. He'd sent a coded message to Kilmer's computer in the early hours of the morning. Kilmer had left instructions to contact at any hour of the day, but Hedgispeth had apparently forgotten that. The message reported that Luther, Hampton, and Alex Deavers all were dead and their corpses incinerated.

Kilmer checked the news database, and sure enough, there had been a "suspicious" break-in at a local garbage-incineration facility in suburban Detroit. The best news was that the kill team had recovered a cache of documents gathered by Luther and Alex Deavers. These documents had been burned along with the bodies.

But none of these were why Kilmer was worried. There were little things. Frank's message seemed too by-the-book, too perfect. But the code used to transmit was verified.

The team was coming in. They were a bit banged up, by their

account. Luther had not gone down without a fight, as Kilmer had expected.

Kilmer was mentally exhausted. This business had taken a lot out of him. He had almost gone to Detroit himself, but that would have raised too much suspicion. He hadn't been in the field in twenty years.

He wondered if any of the others were as worried as he was. Kilmer had kept tabs on those in the Africa Project Group. Most of them were dead now, their legacies taken up by children and successors who knew nothing of their terrible sin.

In retrospect it had been a bad idea to try to backwash Alex Deavers in Africa. Deavers was a lot tougher and luckier than anyone could have imagined. When he survived, the remaining members of the APG panicked and cut off all contact.

"Sir, they're here," said Thomas. His voice sounded a little troubled.

"Let them in," said Kilmer.

Kilmer's door opened, and through it stepped a ghost. Worse for wear but very much alive, Luther Green strode into the boss's office with a look on his face that was both determined and violently angry. Behind him came Hampton, looking better but just as serious. The mystery of how Luther had gotten through security was answered when Adelaide Gibson walked in and closed the door. Unlike the other two, Adelaide did not look angry, but in her hand was a sidearm pointed at the floor.

"Prodigal sons," said Kilmer, his voice grim.

"I wanted to see you before you were arrested," said Luther. "I wanted to ask you something before I bring the wrath of God down on you."

"Agent Gibson," said Kilmer, "I don't suppose that sidearm means you've taken these two into custody."

"You suppose correctly, sir," said Adelaide. "The weapon in my hand is for you. Sir, under Rule 200 I'm going to have to ask you to stand down."

"You?" said Kilmer in disbelief. "You're an overpaid assistant."

"I'm also the agent with the most seniority in the institution. Under Rule 200, I must step in." Adelaide moved toward Kilmer and cocked the weapon. "Inform Security Chief Davis that you are transferring power to me under Rule 200. If you say anything remotely out of line, I'll kill you, sir."

Kilmer complied and verified the order with a security code. Adelaide then told Chief Davis to send a security detail to the director's office.

Hampton searched Kilmer for weapons and found only a small gun the director always carried. He took it from him.

"Adelaide has been suspicious of you for a long time," said Hampton.

"She left me a note warning me not to take the mission," said Luther. "She knew that something wasn't right."

"I did some internal investigating after Luther was given the mission," said Adelaide. "I hacked the company's computers and found out you were covering up something, sir. You broke protocol to get Luther on the case and covered up Alex's mission in Africa by creating a phony internal agency mission."

"If the humiliation is over," said Kilmer, "I'd like to know where my team is."

"They're in the infirmary recuperating. Alive."

"And Alex?" asked Kilmer.

"He didn't make it," said Luther, "so you can add another name to your list of the dead." Luther knew that Alex was alive, but he didn't want anyone at the agency to know. It was his and Hampton's secret.

"I'd like to make a plea to you, Agent Green," said Kilmer. "I assume you've protected the information you and Alex gathered, keeping it somewhere safe. That's fine. You should take it and destroy it and forget about all of this."

Luther let out a short laugh. "You're going to answer for your crimes, and this nation will account for what it has done."

"No," said Kilmer. "I will be killed and the rest of it covered up. You know that."

"He's right," said Adelaide. "It's how things are done."

"Bullshit," said Hampton. "The bastards killed millions of innocent people. Someone has to pay for that."

"Do you know about Rule 225, sir?" asked Luther.

"Of course," said Kilmer.

"Then you know why I will not let this go."

They heard footsteps outside the door. "Security detail," said a man's voice. Adelaide told them to wait.

"I just want to know why you didn't stop it when you could," said Luther. "Why let it go on?"

Kilmer laughed, and it was a sound that was close to madness. "Agent Green, I'm surprised at you. We did nothing because it was working. It got away from us a little, but all in all it was doing what we wanted it to do."

Hampton took a step toward Kilmer and then stopped, realizing that he meant the man bodily harm.

The security detail entered. Kilmer was taken away without a word. They watched as he was carted off in humiliation through the offices.

"What's going to happen now?" asked Luther.

"We'll wait until your information is verified, and then we'll turn him over to a military/CIA panel," said Adelaide.

"And if it doesn't check out?" said Hampton.

"You don't want to think about that," said Adelaide. She put away her weapon and went to Kilmer's desk. "I'm going to call all agents back to Washington for the time being. Luther, you and Hampton have to stay here until this all blows over."

Luther and Hampton shared a look. It had been a long journey, and each saw the exhaustion in the other's eyes. The two men started for the door, knowing that this was just the beginning of their work to make things right again.

Bluemail

Luther was a little nervous as he sat down with the president and his advisers in the Oval Office. The room was filled with faces he'd seen only on CNN and *Meet the Press*. Luther had retrieved both sets of information and presented them to the president in person. The president and his people read the documents in detail, and Luther was then granted this audience.

The president was told the compelling tale of the Wells information and how AIDS had been engineered in the United States. He was also told that Luther was a government consultant who worked outside federal service. The president knew that this was a cover, but he also knew that it was for his own good to accept it.

Luther had been to the White House only once, and then it was under civilian cover. Now the place seemed smaller and more ordinary because of the business he had to attend to. He hoped that he'd leave the place with a fond memory.

"My people tell me that we did not receive all the original documents in these sets of papers from Wells," said the president.

"Yes, sir," said Luther. "I've kept some of them, enough to authenticate the copies I also kept."

"And what is the purpose of that action?" asked a high-ranking presidential adviser.

"I'm protecting my life," said Luther, "as well as the lives of others." He'd been instructed to say as little as possible about the incidents in Detroit.

"This kind of information is too dangerous. We must destroy it and then deal with the people who started this and set things right," said the adviser.

"How will we administer justice for this?" asked Luther.

"We have already made changes at various agencies, and the private companies and military officials responsible that are still with us will be dealt with," said the president.

"How?" asked Luther, and there was a buzz in the room at both his question and his intonation.

"This administration has a lot of respect for you," said the president, "but you do not question me."

"I understand, sir," said Luther. "You're a powerful man, and that's why I've kept a copy of the information—to ensure that your administration keeps its word and delivers justice in this matter. I have the files themselves, as well as other information, stored away."

Now the buzz became a low clamor. The military types in the room looked especially angry.

"Son," said the president, "are you blackmailing the president of the United States?"

"I think of it as 'bluemail,' Mr. President," said Luther. "It's patriotic persuasion for men who understand what a patriot is."

Luther waited to be arrested. The room was quiet, and all eyes were on the president. He leaned back in his chair and glanced up at the ceiling. Then he leaned forward and seemed to think a little more. The military men in the room had the beginnings of smiles on their faces, the kind of smile you wore when you knew someone was about to get taken down.

The president sat up straight and looked Luther directly in the eye. "What are your terms?"

Luther sat on the cold stone of the Lincoln Memorial in the Mall and waited. It was a little chilly out, so he'd worn a light jacket. Tourists stopped by, posing for pictures. He was careful not to get into any of them, although he did take a few snapshots for families.

The mission was finally over for him. He'd had to listen to almost two hours of classical music to put this one behind him. But the melodies had done their job and slowly he was turning back into his old self.

Frank and Kam Lim both returned to active duty, but each held a deep grudge against Luther. Frank seemed particularly upset that his chances for advancement had been hurt.

Adelaide was still in charge of the office and was actually enjoying it. Agents had been sent back out on missions, but Luther and Hampton were given some well-deserved time off.

Luther was proud when he read about the record aid package passed by Congress and the president to fund African AIDS relief and domestic research for a cure. He was even prouder when the federal government handed down indictments against five major corporations and six individuals for violations of federal laws, from RICO to insider trading. Soon thereafter several high-ranking military men suddenly decided to take early retirement.

Sharon and Luther had talked for a long time, trying to make sense out of what had happened. Luther didn't blame her for following orders. She did, however, blame him for acting like such a loner. In her mind he and Hampton might have handled things differently, although she didn't have any idea how they could have done it. In the end they would remain friends, and that was all Luther cared about.

Luther had called home and learned that his family was better. They had worked out a great many things in his absence and had bored a hole into the pain, heartache, and trouble that had built up over the years. He wanted to be there to go back and help, maybe even see Vanessa again. But he'd heard it so many times and now he knew it was true: You could *not* go home again.

Many articles appeared about the recent spate of local terrorism and anti-Arab sentiment in Detroit. Ironically, Nappy's paper, *The Radical,* would have reported something a little more accurate, but since his death it had gone out of business.

Sitting by the monument, Luther checked his watch. It was getting late. He rose and was about to go when he saw a figure approach. He stood still as the man came closer to him. Luther had been coming here almost every night for two weeks, hoping he was right about something.

Alex had mentioned that Rule 225 had been inspired by Lincoln, and then he'd said, *"I'm sure I'll meet Lincoln one day."* It sounded crazy, but Luther knew it was some kind of code. How could you meet Lincoln, unless it was here? So he'd been coming here, hoping to see Alex, but the last few weeks . . . nothing. Alex was probably on some exotic island getting laid and drunk in that order. That had made Luther smile a little.

The man walking toward Luther looked about right, but as he came into better view, Luther saw that it was not Alex but a tall wino in a trench coat. The wino hit him up for a dollar, then ambled off.

"You only encourage them to drink when you do that." It was Alex's voice.

Luther spun around but saw nothing except Honest Abe sitting in his chair.

"I always was a soft touch," said Luther.

"I saw you here last week, but I had to make sure you weren't trying to take me in," said Alex as he stepped into view.

"I understand your concern," said Luther, "but the agency thinks you're dead."

As Alex walked closer, Luther saw that he looked better now. His eyes were clear, and he wore an expression that seemed normal.

"I got myself some proper medical attention," said Deavers. "I think if I keep taking it easy, I might be halfway healthy again."

"It's good to see you," said Luther. He was happy to know that Alex was alive, though he didn't know what the future held for him.

"I see that the government is trying to make amends," said Deavers. "They even rolled a few heads."

"Yes, but it all seems too little too late," said Luther.

"Don't be so pessimistic," said Deavers. "Every good deed has to start somewhere."

"So how about a drink?" asked Luther.

"Sure. It'll go well with the drugs I'm taking."

The two men walked off. Luther wouldn't tell anyone that his friend was still alive. It would be their secret. Maybe this would finally give Alex a chance at a normal life. Luther envied him.

He watched the people taking pictures of the statues in the National Mall. People came here all the time to touch the greatness of America's past leaders. Luther wondered how many people knew how precious the freedom those monuments stood for was to their lives.